"Do you really think they've done away with my poor father?" she sniffed.

He patted her bare rump reassuringly, but told her, "We got to consider it, like it or not. We got to consider that you and even Smithers could be in danger, as well."

She shuddered and said, "Oh, Lord, I never thought of that! Hold me, Custis. Touch me, naughty, and make me forget how cold and cruel the world can be outside your strong loving arms!"

He started to. Then they both stiffened as the night was rent by the sounds of gunshots and breaking glass!

Longarm shoved the girl one way and spun the other as he whirled about, drawing his sixgun. There were two of them. They were both slapping leather and Longarm saw, sickly, that he could only shoot one at a time.

TABOR EVANS

LONGARM

IN THE BIGHORN BASIN

JOVE BOOKS, NEW YORK

LONGARM IN THE BIGHORN BASIN

A Jove Book/published by arrangement with
the author

PRINTING HISTORY
Jove edition/November 1987

ISBN: 0-515-09256-8

Jove Books are published by The Berkley Publishing Group,
200 Madison Avenue, New York, New York 10016.
The name "JOVE" and the "J" logo
are trademarks belonging to Jove Publications, Inc.

10 9 8 7 6 5 4 3 2 1

Chapter 1

The Mile-High City tried to keep abreast of the times. But in truth the Denver Museum of Modern Art was a bit underfunded and modest in size. It tried to make up for this with a genuine plaster of Paris entrance that reminded Longarm of some dreams he'd had after going to bed full of hot tamales and moonshine.

It was almost closing time when the tall federal deputy strode through the imposing plaster portals. But, as luck would have it, a pale comsumptive-looking gal and her escort, who looked as if she could have licked him, were just leaving. They both looked at Longarm as if he needed a shave and some French perfume to make him less country. He was too polite to allow his opinion of *them* to show, so he just looked through them. As they passed he heard the sissy boy whisper, "That chap seems to be wearing a *gun* under that dreadful mail-order tweed!"

Longarm didn't respond to the insult to the store-bought frock coat and pants they made him wear on duty these days. The .44-40 Colt riding his left hip in its cross-draw rig went with the badge he tried to keep out of sight, too. As he got to the main gallery a familiar and less snooty figure hove into view to tell him, "It's closing time, Custis, and if you've come to escort me home the answer is no, you cruel thing."

Longarm smiled sheepishly down at the short, voluptuous honey-blonde who was in charge. "It's my boss, Marshal Vail, you're really sore at," he told her. "But life is too short to waste time arguing with infuriated females. I'm here to get artistic with you this time."

She looked dubious and replied, "If you're talking about some position we somehow missed that wild and wicked weekend, forget it! I wound up bruised!"

Longarm sighed wistfully. "I never expected you to forgive me. I've yet to forgive Billy Vail for sending me out in the field so sudden, even though we *did* head the rascals off. Now they got me after a damned old modernistic artist called Maxwell Windsor. He's managed to vanish himself in delicate if somewhat wild Indian country, along with at least a cartload of his modern paintings. Have you ever heard of the rascal and, better yet, have you got any of his work hung up hereabouts?"

The petite blonde regarded him thoughtfully for a time before she decided, "Your approach wasn't quite that sophisticated the *first* time. But we'd heard nothing about Maxwell Windsor being west of the Mississippi, and you say he's *missing*, Custis?"

Longarm nodded. "Somewhere in the Bighorn Basin, up north. Smack in the middle of the old war grounds of the Crow, Shoshoni and Cheyenne Nations. He come out west this spring to paint the vanishing redman and, next thing anyone knew, him and all his paintings vanished. The B.I.A. has requested me, personal, to look for him up yonder. I know what he looks like. I got a tintype of the greenhorn. I thought, before I headed out after him and his party, I'd best have a look-see at the sort of oil paintings he does. Seeing he's listed as so *moderne,* I was sort of hoping you'd have some of his work on hand."

She still looked suspicious, but said, "As a matter of fact we have just one of his smaller early canvases. I fear his work has become a bit too expensive for our board of trustees of late."

She turned to lead the way along the narrow and now-deserted gallery. Longarm found her rear view admirable but distracting, so he tried to concentrate on the framed oils and watercolors on either side as he followed her. Some of them looked mighty odd. He couldn't figure out what some of them were supposed to picture. As they passed a bright pastel drawing under glass he thought it made a lot more sense than some and said, "Say, I sort of like this one with the racehorse, Miss Vania."

"That's a Degas," she said. "Do tell?" he said. "I'd have swore it was a *thoroughbred.*" For some reason, that made her laugh.

But she remembered she was sore at him as she stopped before a modest-sized total confusion to tell him, "This is the only Maxwell Windsor we have."

Longarm stared at the canvas soberly. *"One* would be more than I'd give house-room to, no offense. You say they pay him *money* for stuff like this? From here it looks as if he just plastered gobs of paint here and there until he'd filled in the frame, for Pete's sake."

Vania sniffed. "He's famous for his palette knife work. You're standing way too close, Custis. Move back with me. That portrait really deserves a bigger room, but we have to make do with what we have."

Longarm saw that she was crawfishing clean across the gallery to stand with her back against the

3

far wall. He shrugged and moved to join her before he turned to cast another critical eye at the thickly daubed canvas. Then he blinked, grinned, and said, "Well I'll be switched."

From that distance, the confusion of raw colors he had seen close-up had resolved into the head and shoulders of a young and mighty pretty gal, likely seated near an open window, with the gloaming light of sunset gleaming on her soft brown hair.

"I see what you mean," he said. "She still looks a mite fuzzy, as if her picture was took through cigar smoke at sunset."

Vania said, "Our catalogue says it's a portrait of his daughter, done when she was about fourteen, about six or seven years ago. Some compare him to Renoir, and . . . But you wouldn't know who I was talking about, would you?"

Longarm replied, "Sure I would. I may be a mite cow, but I ain't stupid. I like this gent's work *better* than Renoir's. Old Renoir makes all gals look soft and young and pretty, but he makes them all look the *same*. Like some ideal gal he's always wanted to meet up with. That picture, yonder, it is the picture of a *real* gal. How in thunder Maxwell Windsor does it with gobs of raw paint at close range eludes me total, but at any *distance* his work looks real as any tinted photograph."

She was staring up at him, bemused, as he kept staring at the missing artist's work. "I take back what I said about him being just a greenhorn," he went on. "If he came west to paint Indians the results would be worth the trouble. You've just helped me a heap, Miss Vania. Now I'll surely know when or if I'm looking at the real thing or just some sign painter's mixing board. The trick is to look at the real thing from a distance. You say even *one* of his paintings is worth real money?"

She nodded. "A lot of money indeed, and you say a lot of his recent work is *missing,* Custis?"

Longarm pursed his lips. "It's mostly Maxwell Windsor himself they want me to locate. But the notion he was last seen with a red river cart full of valuable art sure does open a can of worms to worry about as well. You see, the first thing his friends and relations back east thought of, when he vanished in the Bighorn Basin, was that some fool Indian might not have admired art so much. He was warned them old killing grounds was still a mite unsettled. But he insisted on heading out to paint Crow, Shoshoni, and Cheyenne with no more than a half-breed guide and his own colored valet, aboard a bitty two-wheeled cart, a good six weeks ago. Damn, the Bighorn Basin is mighty big as well as unsettled, and never too friendly."

She asked, "Why would they want to send you out after the lost party *alone,* Custis? Wouldn't it make more sense for the *army* to look for them? The Bighorn is where Custer had all that trouble a few years ago, wasn't it?"

He grimaced. "That was on the *Little* Bighorn, but I reckon the B.I.A. must have been thinking along similar lines when they asked for me by name. Like I said, they got lost sort of delicate. Before we made 'em stop, the Crow, Shoshoni, and the North Cheyenne used to enjoy constant warfare in the Bighorn Basin. This summer the Shoshoni and Cheyenne are more or less at peace and the Crow are on our side, official. The Indian Affairs folk would sort of like to *keep* things that way. The army still feels it owes Mister Lo, the poor Indian, for Custer. Sending out big army patrols who might not be as artistic as me could result in more trouble than one missing artist might be worth. They know I've scouted alongside Crow and fought both Shoshoni and Cheyenne, so—"

"That's insane!" she cut in, swinging about to face him. "If the Indians have attacked an Eastern artist who never did them any harm, what chance would a man like you, who's *fought* with them, have?"

Longarm shrugged and said, "For one thing, since I still have my hair, I may not be as easy for the average Indian to attack as the average greenhorn. Besides, we don't know they got jumped by Indians. Some mighty uncouth whites has moved up that way since the Bighorn range has been thrown open to cows and more alarming critters. How much could an owlhoot get for a mess of Maxwell Windsor paintings, if he was able to recognize 'em as art, up close, Miss Vania?"

She shook her head. "You'd never be able to sell art stolen from a living artist."

Longarm smiled bleakly and said, "I've noticed the works of famous *dead* artists sell for a pretty penny, though. Say we just never find old Maxwell and his red river cart. Say a year or ten from now some fancy dude strolls into a New York gallery with a genuine Maxwell Windsor and almost any story about when and where he came by it?"

She looked horrified. "I wish you hadn't thought of that. Signed and authenticated, his works are worth a lot of money right *now!*"

Longarm nodded soberly. "I sure hope I find him alive, or only scalped, then. I ain't about to find him around *here* in *any* condition. So I thank you for your help, and now I'd best get on down the road, Miss Vania."

As he headed for the front entrance she fell in step with him. "Are you leaving for there at this hour, Custis?"

"I can't. I have to start my search from the Crow Agency, where I can pick up at least two good ponies and mayhaps some directions. To do that, I got to *get* there, and the next northbound Burlington don't leave this side of sunrise."

She said, "Oh, in that case I fail to see why you'd be in such a hurry. I suppose you're seeing some other lady here in Denver these days?"

He was, as a matter of fact, seeing as much of *three* Denver ladies as he could, but he didn't want to seem rude. So he told her, "I hadn't made any plans for this evening. But I thought we'd established that you were sort of vexed with me."

She sniffed. "I was. I mean, I am. I mean, what was that you said about your mean old boss and that sudden trip to Texas, Custis?"

"It was New Mexico. We got an all-points on a bank robbery down Santa Fe way, and Billy sent me to stake out a certain saloon in Taos. *I* thought he was grasping at straws, too, but it worked."

By this time they had made it to the front door. Longarm was expecting her to lock up. But she shut the massive door and locked it from inside. "You might at least have left me a note, you brute."

He said, "Hell, girl, I sent you a postcard from Taos, didn't I?"

"Days later, after I'd cried myself a river and run out of awful things to call you. But since I see, now, it was duty and not *disinterest* that made you break my poor heart . . ."

He had to grab hold of her lest they both fall to the floor as she proceeded to climb his frame. He heard the sharp pop of someone's button and told her, "Take it easy, little darling. I know this is an art museum and I've always found nude studies mighty interesting, but . . . on a marble floor?"

"There's a leather chesterfield in my office," she purred.

So he raced her there, and she not only won, but had managed to strike a mighty interesting nude pose by the time he could get his boots off.

Chapter 2

Longarm would have found the train ride tedious even if he hadn't boarded the northbound local somewhat fatigued by Vania's all-night art lesson. There was no direct line to the Bighorn Indian Agency. He had to transfer a couple of times and detour all over Robin Hood's barn to turn what should have been about an eight- or ten-hour ride into an all-day scenic excursion through some mighty uninteresting scenery.

They had enjoyed a wetter than usual green-up a month or so back, but the summer sun and mummified winds of the High Plains had already commenced to brown the rolling prairie all around and droop the heads of such livestock as they rattled past.

Longarm didn't feel that old, but when he'd first come west, after the War, it had all been buffalo country this far north. Most of the longhorns who had it now looked as if they would be willing to give it back to the buffalo. But the grass and water was in fact better up this way, despite the ferocious way the winds played with the temperature from day to day or even hour to hour. Longarm knew it would be after sundown by the time he got off at the Crow Agency. So while he was seated in his shirtsleeves by an open window, and still feeling flushed, he had a sheepskin coat and winter chaps lashed to his old army saddle, perched above him on a too-narrow luggage rack. A man had to keep his possibles close to hand when they made him change from one fool day coach to another all day. His folded frock coat and battered Stetson rode beside him on the empty half of the hardwood seat, along with most of the magazines he had picked up at the Denver depot that morning. He had long since read them all. Like many a self-educated man, Longarm read faster, as well as more, than some might think. He'd always felt a mite wistful about the way the War had cut his already modest education short. So he tried to make up for it by reading just about anything.

But the time he was browsing at the moment, as his last local slowly rattled and rolled the last leg of his journey, was not the sort of reading material he would have picked up just to kill an hour or so. For Vania, bless her artistical bottom, had pressed it on him as a parting present, insisting that if it didn't help, it might at least remind him of her.

It did. There were lots of nude studies in the thick catalogue of modern art she had stolen from the museum for him. Not many seemed as well-built as Vania. For some reason the gents Vania called advanced guards or whatever seemed to like to paint gals old and fat and ugly or so skinny and boyish it hardly seemed worth the trouble of undressing them. The thick book itself was printed on heavy stock. The pictures were sepia photoprints, pasted in by hand to fit the captions. Now and again Longarm got a mild chuckle out of a naked lady captioned as a still-life or a bowl of fruit entitled "Sunset Along the Hudson."

Most of the pictures seemed to have been put in right, though. Longarm had decided he liked the pictures of a gent called Thomas Eakins best, even if they did call him a modernist, whatever that meant. Old Tom painted modern scenes, mostly along some river back East, but he painted old-fashioned enough so a body knew what in thunder he was *looking* at. There was one picture, of a gent rowing a racing shell in his undershirt, that looked good enough to pass for a photograph. For some reason, the artistic gent who'd written the book seemed to think this was what was *wrong* with Eakins.

They were kinder to Maxwell Windsor, the painter Longarm had been sent to search for. Longarm had to whistle as he noted the prices set for some of Windsor's oils or even watercolors. Photographed at the right distance, and then in only one brown tone, the reproductions in the catalogue didn't look as sloppy as Windsor really worked with a glorified putty knife. He didn't go in for naked ladies. He mostly painted—or plastered—landscapes and portraits. He liked to pose folk against interesting landscapes, and Longarm had to agree that would have been the way he'd have done it. One old gal was sort of ugly, but there was a mighty pretty waterfall in back of her to make up for it.

Vania had marked the pages dealing with the missing artist with a newspaper clipping. He was glad she had a brain as well as other charms. For, while the heavy catalogue hadn't told him one thing he hadn't already known about Maxwell Windsor, the column a sarcastic art critic had written about him explained a lot.

Windsor had done most of the work he was famous for back East, mostly along the Hudson River of New York State. But while they weren't in

11

the catalogue, he had last held a showing of what he claimed to be a lasting tribute to the vanishing West.

Longarm glanced out the window. A hell of a lot of West was still there. But, the column went on, *Windsor's* West had been a real bust. He'd been savaged by the critics of "Impressionism" for giving a mighty poor impression of any part of the West *they'd* ever seen. They said he'd gotten the "light" all wrong, and that an Indian pueblo painted misty against a soft lavender sky looked silly, when everyone knew how raw and razzle-dazzle the sunlight of the Great American Desert always was.

Longarm found that a mite unfair. He had been down in the pueblo country during a rainy spell, and the desert sky could turn lavender or just about any other color one could think of along about sundown. But the way they had ridiculed the gent about the way he made up Western scenery no doubt accounted for his sudden desire to do it *right*. The column said some had found fault with Windsor's "Impressions" of Indians as well. He had sure headed for the right place to paint real Indians. What else he had run into in the Bighorn Basin was still unknown.

Longarm closed the catalogue on the clipping and put it aside. Vania had asked him to bring it back. It was sort of heavy to lug all over. Maybe he'd be able to leave it for safekeeping at the Crow Agency, if he ever got there.

The sun was low outside, and as a matter of fact the sky to the east, at least, *was* getting sort of lavender. Longarm got out his pocketwatch to check against his crumpled railroad timetable. He didn't curse out loud. He was glad he hadn't when a soft female voice asked permission to sit down beside him.

Longarm glanced up, blinked, and hastily made room by shoving everything on the seat beside him into a compact bundle against the aisle-side arm rest. He was no fool. That left just enough room for the pretty little thing to sit down beside *him,* close. Her perfume smelled expensive, although she'd been sweating some of late under the tan poplin travel duster she had on over whatever. From the way her soft hip felt against his when she sat down, it wasn't much. She had a small straw boater pinned atop her upswept hair, which was shiny black where coal ash hadn't settled. Her pert nose was beauty-marked by fly ash as well. He wondered if he'd have thought she looked like Renoir had made her up if he hadn't been studying art so much lately.

Like the pretty French gals Renoir went in for, she was pretty in a sort of soft negative way. Like a window dummy, her beauty was more a lack of anything *wrong* with her features, rather than anything a man could outright say he *admired.* But her voice was sort of interesting, if not seductive, as she leaned closer and told him, "I know you must think I'm behaving oddly, sitting down so boldly by a gentleman I've not been introduced to."

He had noticed there were plenty of empty seats all about. But he'd been raised polite. So he just said, "I'd best introduce me to you, then, ma'am. My name is Custis Long."

She dimpled, confided she was Lotta Cranston, and asked how soon they'd be getting to Sheridan, Wyoming Territory.

He said, "Less than twenty minutes, Lord willing and the creeks don't rise."

She looked relieved. "Thank heavens. *You'll* be getting off there, too, won't you?" she asked.

He repressed a wistful sigh. "Not hardly. I know Sheridan is the end of the line for most folk, but I got to ride an hour or so up the line to the Crow Agency."

She sighed and said, "Oh, dear, I don't know what I'll do, in that case."

He regarded her thoughtfully. "What's the problem? Luggage? I'll be proud to unload you if them two porters riding this fool train with us downright refuse you, Miss Lotta."

"That's not my problem. There's another man aboard who's been pestering me ever since I got on at Edgemont. I don't have anyone meeting me at Sheridan and, should he follow me off, there . . ."

Longarm nodded soberly. "Some gents just don't know how to act around a lady traveling alone. Can you point the poor brute out to me, Miss Lotta?"

She shook her head. "He didn't follow me into this car, thank heavens. He was trying to . . . you know . . . pick me up in the club car just now. As I left, he followed. I confess I was almost running by the time I reached this car, saw an obvious gentleman seated alone, and threw myself on his mercy. I guess that other man saw how much bigger you were and turned back at the doorway."

Longarm twisted his head to see nothing much back that way before he said, "He might not have been too serious in his intent. I can't look that big, sitting down and facing the other way. But if you'd like me to have a word with him about his manners I can look big enough, wearing my *growly* face. Shall we take us a stroll towards the club car?"

She shuddered and gasped, "Oh, no, I couldn't allow myself to be the cause of a *scene*. I'm on my way to Sheridan to take up a teaching position. How would it look to the school board if I arrived with two men fighting over me?"

Longarm chuckled. "In all modesty, a fight wasn't what I had in mind. Like I said, I can growl pretty good, and the man has to be fairly harmless if he quit

14

so easy. When we get to Sheridan I'll see you safe to the platform. That ought to do it."

"What if it doesn't?" she asked. "You just said that's where *he's* likely to be getting off, too!"

"Well, you hop right into a rig, alone, and ask the driver to take you direct to your hotel—"

She cut in, "I don't know which hotel, if any, I'd want to stay at in Sheridan. I've never been there before. It's almost dark outside now, and...Oh, what shall I ever *do?*"

As if to upset her further, the conductor came through just then to announce, "Sheridan. Next stop Sheridan, and we won't *be* there long."

The gal beside him looked like she was clouding up to bust out crying. Longarm called out to the conductor. The older man smiled in recognition and came over. Longarm told him, "I'll bet you a dollar you couldn't drop my saddle and possibles off at the Crow Agency when you get there, Gus."

"You lose," Gus said, "but you could lose that McClellan and Winchester as well, if they hit the platform amongst all them Indians without you, Longarm."

Longarm nodded thoughtfully but rose to shove the art catalogue into a saddlebag as he drew the Winchester from its scabbard in exchange, muttering, "I doubt any Indian, eating regular, would steal anything more serious than this gun, Gus. Just drop the rest off and, should anyone ask, I'll be joining my possibles directly."

By this time the girl had risen to step out into the aisle. Longarm put on his hat and coat as he asked her where her luggage might be.

She held up her big but not-that-big purse to explain, "I sent my trunks on ahead and caught a later train. I simply couldn't see getting up that early this morning."

The conductor told them to sort it out as best they could, and moved on to alert other passengers getting off as the train began to chuff a mite slower.

Longarm took Lotta's arm and escorted her to the forward platform of their day coach. She told him he was a real gent to go to so much trouble for a lady. He knew he was, but he just said, "There won't be nothing all that important I can do up at the Crow Agency after dark. I can bunk for the night just as good or better, here in town, then catch a dawn-run on up the line. Meanwhile, we'll get you settled in safe and sound. I don't want to upset you needlessly, Miss Lotta, but do you see that *other* gent before I notice him, you'd best point him out to me. I'd hate to slap leather on a man who only aimed to ask me for a light."

When the train finally hissed to a stop and Longarm was able to help her down, the only other passengers getting off seemed to be taken. There were half a dozen other men moving about on the station platform in the tricky light of the gathering darkness, but they all had other women and some even kids with them. When Longarm commented on this, she said, "I know. He must still be on the train."

The train was starting up again even as they spoke. Longarm could have made it back aboard, and seriously considered it, before he wondered why any man with a lick of sense and a pretty gal clinging to his arm would want to do a thing like that.

The odds were fifty-fifty he'd wind up with a handshake and sincere thanks. On the other hand, the evening was young.

As the modest crowd began to thin and Longarm got his bearings on the lights of downtown Sheridan, he said, "The best place for us . . . I mean *you,* would be the Grand Paris Hotel. It ain't all that grand and anyone can see we ain't in Paris, but the last time I

16

was here I didn't really need this Winchester for the mice."

She gasped, "Oh, do they really have mice?"

He told her, "They got to have something, and mice mean neither rats nor roaches. That's because mice eat roaches and rats eat mice and, hey, I'm just funning. I didn't see nothing serious the last time I stayed at the Grand Paris Hotel."

She sighed and said it was all in his hands now. So he took one of her elbows in his left hand and led her toward the light, holding his Winchester down polite in his right hand.

As they reached the end of the platform, she surprised him mildly by stopping dead in her tracks. But, as he swung around to see why, he saw she had taken a big white kerchief from her purse.

A lady wanting to blow her nose seemed reasonable enough. But when she dropped the filmy white cloth to the splintered planks between them it didn't. So, as the first pistol flash from the darker side of the platform put a hot lead slug through the space Longarm had been standing in beside her, Longarm wasn't there any more.

He yelled, "Hit the planks, damn it!" even as he levered a round into the chamber of his saddle gun to follow his own good advice and keep rolling. His invisible attacker tore a long, dry sliver of pine from the platform next to Longarm's face as he fired back at the flash, heard a kicked-dog yelp of pain, and fired again for luck and by guess.

He figured he'd guessed right when he heard his target cry out, "I give! I give! Oh . . . Mother, make it stop!"

Sheridan was a good-sized town by Wyoming standards. Even as Longarm moved in on the one he'd downed, he could hear others headed their way, in considerable numbers, attracted by the sound of gunfire as moths are to a candle flame. Longarm had never met a smart moth, either.

He circled to get his own back to the prairie darkness and thus made out the form of the man he had downed against the dim light. The rascal was stretched out on the railroad ballast with one leg hooked over a rail. Longarm hunkered down for a word with him, observing, "You figure to get run over by the next train through. But that's what friends are for, and I feel sure you want me to make friends with you now, right?"

The man didn't answer. Longarm felt the side of his throat and then patted him down for I.D. There didn't seem to be any. He'd been hit low in the gut and high in the chest. Longarm stood up again to see what else might be going on. He strode over to the edge of the platform, which came to his waist with his feet on the ground, and placed the Winchester politely on the planking as he heard some distant voice proclaiming itself the law and baying at the moon for some explanation of all the recent noise.

Just beyond his saddle gun, Lotta Cranston or whoever she was had not yet risen from where she lay prone on the platform a few feet from her treacherous white kerchief. Longarm told her, "Your boyfriend won't be slinging no more lead our way. But you'd best come up with a more sensible story than the one you've been slinging at me. For I am the law, too, as they no doubt told you before they sent you to set me up for a twilight tryst that wasn't supposed to turn out just this way."

She didn't answer. Longarm reached across his Winchester to feel the wrist attached to her limp left arm. When he felt no pulse he sighed and said, "I *told* you to *duck,* girl. Meeting up with you has just been one infernal letdown after another. For now I

18

still don't see why anyone wanted to go to so much trouble to stop me, from doing whatever. It has to be something a lot more important than looking for a lost greenhorn."

Chapter 3

Sheridan was a county seat as well as a fair-sized cattle and coal-mining town. Their coroner had a small but up-to-date autopsy theater attached to the municipal morgue. Longarm was chewing the end of an unlit cheroot to settle his own innards as the gruff old coroner and his pretty little woman assistant poked about in Miss Lotta's.

The naked body of the man he had downed at the depot lay on yet another zinc table, waiting to be stitched back together with butcher's twine. They had done him first because Longarm had admitted to putting at least two rounds of .44-40 in him. Longarm had seemed less surprised than they had when they'd wound up with exactly two .44-40 slugs in their bitty tin dish. He didn't know how concerned he really felt about other ballistic evidence until the coroner hauled a bloody ball of lead out of the dead gal's torso to proclaim, ".45 Volcano. Same sort of rounds that *other* rascal favored. Don't ask me why. Nobody has any business going up against a Winchester with a single-action thumb buster."

The young gal said, "At least she never knew

21

what hit her. A ball that size through the sternum knocks one out directly, does it hit the heart or not."

The coroner grimaced and added, "In this case it did. She must have been facing him with her back to you when she was hit. I'd say that lets you off the hook as far as *she* might be concerned, Deputy Long. We've still got to put something sensible about the two rounds you put in *him*. I know you're a lawman and it's obvious he was shooting back at you. After that it gets a mite murky, no offense. You say you never saw him before and that he just up and pegged a mess of pistol shots your way, in tricky light? I'd sure feel better if you had at least one *witness* to the fray, old son."

Longarm said, "We got one. *Me*. Why in thunder would I fib to you about an open-and-shut attempt to assassinate a peace officer?"

The older man didn't answer. He stared thoughtfully down at the naked lady stretched out between them. Even cold and dead, anyone could see she'd been a beauty many a man would consider worth fighting over. The coroner sort of nodded to himself and then he mused aloud, "Let's see if I've got this straight. A deputy on his way to an Indian reserve a good sixty miles up the line meets a pretty stranger on a train. He naturally decides to get off *here* with her, instead?"

Longarm was painfully aware of the way the young assistant across the table was looking at him. He scowled and told them both, "She suckered me off the train with a story about needing protection from some cuss who'd been trying to bother her."

The dishwater blonde regarding the remains of another pretty gal nodded soberly and murmured, "That's how we defend ourselves from forward gents, all right. The first thing I always do when a man gets fresh with me is to get fresh with another."

Her boss shushed her with a frown. "It's been known to happen. But how do you know this gal wasn't being pestered by the very gent you shot it out with, once all three of you got off that train?"

Longarm shook his head. "He never got off. I was on the prod and watching for that. He was staked out here to gun me."

"But you say you was on your way to the Crow Agency, not here."

"That's why they put this gal aboard after I'd left Denver! Her job was to make sure I got off here at Sheridan, where a hired white gun could murder me and fade discreetly into your considerable white population. That dead gent, yonder, must not have known me on sight. If he had, there'd have been no need for the gal to signal him with her kerchief, and I might not have been so lucky this evening."

The only girl alive in the room asked, "How did you know it was a signal when this poor thing simply dropped her kerchief?"

Longarm looked disgusted and replied, "Because she had no other reason for doing so. As you just so kindly pointed out, she'd *already* picked me up. Let the record show I didn't fire first. But, yeah, I sensed I was in trouble and got to moving sudden as soon as I saw her spreading icing on the cake."

Both medical examiners looked confused. So Longarm went on to explain, "She was cooler under pressure than her sidekick. But I'm paid to be nosy, so I'd caught her in a fib or more even before she made that last sneaky move. She either lied about where she'd boarded the train or why she did so with no luggage. She said she'd sent the luggage on ahead to avoid getting up early. That made no sense at all. Even if I'd believe a gal could be dumb enough to get up early so she could check her possibles aboard an earlier train in order to go back to bed, she got on

23

at Edgemont well after noon, and when we got *here*, she said nothing about picking up said luggage."

"Maybe she would have, had she lived a mite longer," the coroner suggested.

Longarm shook his head. "She didn't *have* any infernal luggage. She just made something up sudden when I asked, on the train, and then forgot it as she commenced to act lost in your big city. She said she was on her way here to be a schoolmarm, only nobody was meeting her train and she had no notion where to spend the night, *knowing* she would arrive after sundown."

The blonde assistant nodded. "Right. She picked you up planning to stay the night with you."

Longarm looked sheepish. "Not hardly, even if I do look weak-natured. Her job was to set me up for a killer and no doubt catch the next train out, feeling more smart than sorry about what fools we mortals be."

The old coroner sighed and said, "I'll allow your theory works, old son. But that's all it is—a theory. There's not a lick of evidence to indicate this dead lady knew that dead gent or vice versa. I fear we may have to impanel a full jury to decide the exact facts, here."

Longarm groaned. "Aw, come on. I'm already running late on more serious federal business, Doc."

But the older official insisted, "It was your own notion to stop off here for a gunfight, Deputy. As to your mission, as I understand it, you're trying to locate one or more men who may be dead or alive at the moment. Meanwhile, I got two corpses for *certain* to account for properly, and we like to do everything nice and proper in Sheridan County. I'll allow, off the record, that the panel will likely believe your unsupported story, since you do have a federal badge backing your word. But it would be downright

24

sloppy to let you wander off without a lick of sworn testimony."

"Can't I just leave a sworn deposition?" Longarm tried.

Before the coroner could say no, the town constable Longarm had met earlier over by the tracks came in to say, "Well, we got us a name for the dead gent, now. Thanks to that missing finger on his left hand and the interesting scar down the right side of his fool face, the Texas Rangers has been kind enough to verify by wire that he stacks up as the late Icehouse Ike Cranston. Texas don't want him, but the Rangers was keeping an eye on him. Seems he was fired as a town constable a while back for gunning drunks above and beyond the call of duty. Texas can't prove it, but the word on the rascal was that his gun was for hire, cheap."

The blonde assistant gasped and said, "But this dead woman, here, gave her *own* last name as Cranston!"

Longarm nodded. "She could have been his wife. On the other hand, she could have had a nasty sense of humor. Had things gone as planned, it hardly mattered *who* she told me she was."

The town law said, "If the late Icehouse Ike was married up lawful, there'll be a record of it some infernal place. You want me to get back to Western Union on that, Doc?"

The coroner shook his head. "The county's already spent enough of the taxpayers' money on this foolishness. Since we've established the male cadaver as a suspected Texas gunslick with no damned business in Wyoming, and the female cadaver as someone who knew him at least well enough to use his last name as her own, I reckon a sworn deposition from Deputy Long, here, ought to do it. He is the law, after all, and I'll be switched with snakes if anything *else* fits better than his version of what happened."

So an hour and a half later Longarm would have been free to go on up the line, had any trains been headed that way before morning. The pretty coroner's assistant turned out to be spoken for, and he'd been fibbing to Lotta when he'd told her he'd never really seen any mice at the Grand Paris Hotel.

But it was still the best hotel he knew of in Sheridan, so that was where he headed. He hired a room next to the communal bathroom on the top floor. Then, since sleeping in a strange bed alone was sort of tedious even when one felt tired, he wandered into the hotel taproom to see if there was anything he could do to cheer the room he'd hired up.

He knew the odds against sudden friendships in strange towns this late on a weekday night. But he'd missed supper, and a beer or more might at least calm his nerves enough to turn in early.

The kitchen was still open, according to the waitress, so he let her lead him to a booth across from the bar and told her he'd admire his eggs on chili con carne.

"I can see by the crush of your hat you must be a Colorado rider," she said. "You know, of course, how they cook chili north of the Arkansas Divide?"

He smiled up at her. "I know a couple of places in Denver where they don't stint on the peppers. But now that you mention it, we do seem a mite north of the border. What *else* would you suggest, ma'am?"

"You can call me Kitty and the Chink out back makes a tolerable beef hash. I can ask him to pepper it extra for you. That's what you'd get if you ordered chili con carne, in any case."

Longarm laughed and told her they had a deal. The good old gal was not very attractive, but he could see she had a good heart.

26

She asked what he wanted to drink with his meal. He said a pitcher of draft beer sounded about right. She fetched him the beer from the bar before she headed back to the kitchen to get the rest of his order. He wasn't sure whether she always walked that way or not. Either way, she sure wasted a lot of wiggle. It gave him something to ponder as he lit a cheroot and tried to relax. For while every man knew, at a glance, whether a gal was ugly or pretty, it was a mite harder to sort out the exact reasons. Longarm recalled reading someplace that history might have turned out different if Cleopatra's nose had been one inch longer or Bloody Mary's waistline had been only a few inches trimmer. Poor old Kitty was ugly in as mysterious a way as the late Lotta Cranston had been pretty. It was nothing in particular one could point to. By the time she was coming back with his grub he was staring her way with so much interest that she started blushing. He quickly tore his eyes away from her dubious charms, lest she get the wrong idea, but the damage had been done. He had to compliment her on the steaming plate of hash and eggs she set before him. When she moved over to the end of the bar to chat with the sleepy-looking barkeep, Longarm became painfully aware of the arch looks she kept casting his way as he ate and drank, faster than he might have with a clearer conscience. He hated to be led on, himself, so it seemed sort of cruel to think so poorly of a gal who obviously admired him a heap.

Longarm liked to top off a late snack with apple pie, cheese, and coffee. But he'd made up his mind to quit while he was ahead and compensate Kitty with a decent tip, and he would have, had not Kim Stover chosen that very minute to come in from the lobby, stare at him, and exclaim, "Custis Long! What on earth are you doing here in Sheridan?"

He rose politely as she joined him. He said he was just as surprised but not at all upset to bump into her.

She didn't look as sure, even though she sat down across from him. She had to. She'd been raised polite and they had known one another intimately for some time, in the Biblical as well as social sense.

Kim Stover was a beautiful widow woman from the Bitter Creek country. She ran a hell of a lot of cows and had a hell of a lot of money in the bank. After that it got worse. She'd once made the mistake of asking Longarm to marry her and, although she'd accepted his explanations like the good sport she was, he suspected she had never really forgiven him.

As the waitress came over, shooting daggers at Kim Stover, Longarm said, "The hash here is mighty fine, Kim." Then he got to feel as if *he* wasn't much, as the rich and somewhat expensively dressed young widow woman smiled sweetly and told Kitty she'd have tea, toast, and a small bowl of mushroom soup.

As the waitress flounced off, looking hurt, Longarm smiled across the table. "I see you're still worried about your figure, Kim," he said.

She smiled back and declared, "No, I'm not. By the time a woman has to *worry* about her figure it's usually too *late*. I haven't been getting to ride as often as when...we first met. This current beef boom can't last forever, and I've been branching out some. I'm here in Sheridan to look into the local coal pits. They tell me it's good coal, and as long as I already own my own fleet of freight cars—"

He cut in to say, "I always said you'd wind up rich. If I don't get shot before I've put in my time with Justice, I may be able to afford a garden and indoor plumbing on my pension."

She looked away. "Let's not go into that again, Custis. It's a good excuse. We both know the real reason you pack a badge and a gun is that you just

28

can't see living any other way. Are you staying at this hotel?"

"Yep. Room 307. What room might *you* be in, Kim?"

She lowered her lashes and said, "I don't think I want to tell you. You know I'm as weak-willed as you, and it always hurts so much, afterwards."

He nodded and said, "I've noticed. You may be right. I'll only be here this one night, anyway. Of course, a lot can happen in one night, but—"

"We'd better change the subject," she cut in, tossing him a too-bright smile as she added, "You still haven't told me what they sent you up this way to do, dear."

He could take a hint, so he told her about his mission. She tried to pretend she was interested. "I don't envy you, hunting stray dudes over in the Bighorn Basin with the trail a good six weeks cold. That's a lot of open range you're talking about, you know."

He shrugged and said, "That's what I tried to tell Billy Vail. How well might *you* know that range, Kim?"

She didn't get to answer, just yet. The poor ugly waitress had come back to slam her order down sort of rudely. Kim just thanked her and waited until she'd flounced back to glare at them from the end of the bar before she picked up her spoon and told Longarm, "I've herded beef through it, up to the copper country for the miners. Small herds, of course, so we didn't have any real trouble."

"What sort of trouble might *bigger* herds have over that way, Kim? I thought the Indians had calmed down some in recent times."

She washed down a nibble of toast with a sip of tea. "Cattle thieves are more of a problem in the basin since Uncle Sam taught Mister Lo some manners. The Crow have never been much of a bother and they say the only Cheyenne left in these parts are over on the Tongue River this summer."

He nodded and said, "Yeah, that would be Little Wolf's band. He ain't supposed to be there, but they can't get him to stay anyplace else, so they're ignoring him, official, as long as he behaves himself. The Tongue is a good piece from the Bighorn Basin, and Little Wolf has always been reasonable, for a Cheyenne. Now, if I could just figure out why *cattle* thieves would want to mess with an artistical dude ... You say they left you and a modest-sized outfit alone, Kim?"

She nodded and said, "The way I hear it, most of the outlaws over in that basin are just cowboys gone wrong, not out-and-out highway robbers. They're out to get rich, not to pick fights for small profit. They left us alone because they could see it would have been what Mister Lo calls a bad fight. Win or lose, they wouldn't have gotten enough beef to make it worth the risk."

Longarm sipped some beer and mused aloud, "Even a small herd of beef has to be worth more than a red river cart filled with nothing but art and art supplies. The basin is big and sort of bumpy, and we did have a wet spring about the time the dudes wandered in there. How do you feel about a flash flood catching them down in some distant draw, Kim?"

She shrugged. "It wouldn't be the first time greenhorns camped in a dry wash that suddenly got wet. But didn't you say that artist had hired a guide, dear?"

Longarm grimaced. "I talk too much. Nobody can tell me much about Windsor's guide, save that he's some sort of breed. I can't come up with any nation that manages to drown regular on the High Plains. I can come up with all sorts of accidents even an old

30

hand could have in such rough country. But unless all three of them got accidented the same way at the same time, by now some survivors should have reported in."

Kim asked, "What if Mr. Windsor, himself, got hurt or took sick? Might not his hirelings have decided just to ride off with his supplies and such?"

Longarm shook his head. "Anything's possible, but that hardly seems likely. For one thing, we're talking about canvas, paint, and camping gear, not treasure. For another thing, at least one of the gents he took along was a personal servant who'd been with him some time. He'd have to be mighty dumb as well as unusually treacherous if he couldn't see Windsor's kith and kin would likely reward him for even *bad* news of his boss."

She didn't really look too interested as she said it was all beyond her. So he didn't bother to tell her about the shootout he'd had earlier. He couldn't see how it fit, either. He let her have her own turn to speak. He wondered if she really gave a damn about Wyoming coal, either. He could see she was just talking about things that might not matter to keep the conversation off matters that might. He knew the dangers of stirring up the ashes of bittersweet memories. But, damn, she was still so *pretty*.

As she ran on, he found himself trying to decide just why she was prettier than, say, that poor old-mousy Kitty glaring at them from the corner. For openers, pretty gals hardly ever glared. After that, the differences got harder to fathom. When you got right down to it, tits were tits, lips were lips, and eyes were what a gal looked at you with. He didn't want to ponder the more intimate parts of *any* gal right now, facing the rest of the night alone. Kim had his own privates tingling, just talking about shipping coal. He knew she was likely beginning to suffer the same way when she suddenly left half her sup and tea untasted to tell him, "Forgive me, Custis, it's been grand talking to you again, but I've a splitting head-ache and an early business appointment, so, if you'll forgive me . . ."

He got to his feet just ahead of her, saying, "I can see you look sort of throwed and stomped, Kim. You just go on ahead and I'll settle up here."

She insisted, "Oh, I'd rather pay my own bill, dear."

But he shook his head. "I know you would. That's one reason we never spent much time together, Kim."

She gasped, blushed, and turned to almost dash out of the taproom as Longarm sat back down with a sigh. The ugly waitress moved almost as fast getting over to his booth. She asked if there was anything else she could do for him. He smiled wistfully and said, "Yeah. I'd sure like a big slab of apple pie, cheddar cheese if you got it, and some black coffee. You'd best bring the pot. I don't figure on sleeping much, tonight, and it feels better if you're wide awake."

Chapter 4

When he struck a match to light the lamp by his bed, upstairs, something gray and fuzzy ducked out of the light. It hadn't been big enough to worry about. But he hadn't realized, until he saw how empty even a small hotel room could look, that he'd been sort of hoping to find someone more interesting than a *mouse* waiting for him.

He peeled off his coat and tossed it across the foot of the big brass bedstead, muttering, "Mayhaps it's just as well. I got an early train to catch and I'd hate to have to feel this awful *tomorrow* night, in any case."

He hung up his hat and gun rig, stripped off his vest, and took his derringer from a vest pocket to tuck under the mattress at the head of the bed. The derringer was attached by a gilt chain to his pocket-watch. He didn't want to know what time it might be. He'd killed some time, but not nearly enough, down in the taproom after Kim had left.

He sat on the bed to dig out the notes he had on the missing party and lay back to go through them once again. It didn't work. It was hard to work up interest, reading stuff you knew by heart. There was no mystery about where Maxwell Windsor had come from and there wasn't even a hint as to where he might have vanished.

He finally gave up and, sincerely sorry he'd swilled so much coffee downstairs, undressed and trimmed his lamp to see if counting sheep could be any more tedious. It worked out about even. He wouldn't have been really tired after an all day sit-down even if he hadn't liked his coffee strong and black.

So he was still wide awake when he heard soft, mysterious clicks and rose on one bare elbow to cock his head and mutter, "Cut it out, mouse."

A mouse might have heard his soft growl. Whoever was trying to pick his door lock hadn't. As he heard another soft, metallic scrape, Longarm tossed the covers off, swung his bare feet to the bare floorboards, and rose in the dark to reach for the more serious .44-40 sixgun hanging handy.

He moved silent as an Indian horse thief to the door and, as he could see his would-be visitor was stopped by the hotel key Longarm had left in the lock on his side, he quietly removed it and tossed it on the bed to see what might happen next.

What happened next was that the door, of course, came unstuck and proceeded to open. The hall lamp outside had been put out for the night, either by the hotel staff to save coal oil or just as likely by someone else who didn't want to be outlined as he opened doors with a skeleton key.

Longarm figured it was about time he took someone alive to have a serious chat with. He raised his revolver to rabbit-punch whoever the intruder might be. But just as he was set to swing he heard a soft female whisper, and whispered back, "You should have knocked, honey. I was just about to clobber you, for Pete's sake!"

She gave a startled gasp, but still managed to keep her own voice barely audible as she replied, "Good heavens, you do get around *quiet* in the dark, don't you?"

He said, "Yeah, a lady's rep is always safe with me." Then he reached out to haul her in for a hug and a kiss with his gun-filled fist in the small of her back and his free hand roaming more freely over her dressing gown. She naturally wrapped him in her own arms and as they came up for air she giggled and whispered, "Oh, you're stark naked! I guess you knew I just had to come to you, didn't you?"

He kissed her again, said the thought had never crossed his mind, and added, "Speaking of coming, why don't we get out of this ridiculous vertical position and do it right?"

She giggled as he swept her off her feet, carried her to the bed, and lowered her to the mattress. When he joined her in bed she was still wearing the robe.

Some gals were like that. It had been a spell since last old Kim had begged for more by the dawn's rosy light, so he kissed her as he fumbled with the knotted sash of her robe. He couldn't get it untied with his one free hand, but as she was wearing nothing under it he decided they could manage the first awkwardness without possibly awkward fumblings, so he just opened her robe as wide as he could, where it really mattered, and whispered, "Powder River and let her buck!" as he entered her sweet flesh. She gasped as if she'd been expecting him to do anything else, which was sort of silly on her part, considering. Then she giggled again, wrapped her smooth bare legs around his waist, and crooned, "Oh, yesss! I admire a man

35

who don't shilly-shally, and I'd forgotten just how lovely this could feel!"

He commenced to move faster as he kissed the base of her throat and growled, "Jesus, I'd about given up this notion, Kim." She sobbed, "I was *trying* to be good, downstairs, but life is so short and some nights are so long. Keep your voice down, darling. These walls are so thin and the rooms on either side are booked."

He chuckled and whispered, "It's a good thing you remember room numbers so good. I'd hate to think of you doing this with anyone *else* right now!"

She started to say something that might have been more sensible, and then she was climaxing, and if the guests on either side didn't hear her moans and groans of rapture, they had to be stone-deaf.

He spread her thighs wider with an elbow hooked under either knee to finish right and this inspired her to untie her sash and fling her robe wide open to haul him down against her naked, perky breasts as she sobbed, "Oh, God, I'm coming again!"

That made two of them. As he lay limp atop her she ran her loving hands down his bare back to dig her nails gently into his bare buttocks and murmur, "That was divine. But I fear I'm still not satisfied. It's been so long and . . . My, you *are* still nice and long. Would you mind if I got on top, dear?"

He laughed and pointed out he'd never minded before. So, as they swapped positions, she shucked her robe entire and proceeded to ride him as gleefully as she gasped, "Oh, it feels even deeper this way, Mr. Custer."

He thrust his hips almost three times before that sunk in and he muttered, "How did *Custer* get into this, Kim?"

She replied, "Silly, my name is Kitty, not Kim, and didn't that other gal downstairs call you Custer?"

Longarm gulped, said, "Not hardly," and wondered why it still felt so good, considering this was the wrong gal.

He suppressed a roar of laughter as it sank in fully. She stopped bouncing to just sit and throb teasingly as she asked him what was so funny. He said, "Don't stop *now*, for Gawd's sake. I ain't laughing at *you*. I'm laughing at *me!*"

She leaned forward to tease his chest with her swaying nipples as she giggled and replied, "I feel mighty happy, too. I was so afraid you meant to meet that other gal upstairs, later. I could tell she didn't want you as much as I did. But I'll have to allow she was a mite better-looking than me."

Longarm rolled her on her back. She sure *felt* lovely in the dark as she writhed her naked, passionate flesh against his all the way to glory.

She was surprised but didn't seem displeased when he stayed put, nibbling her ear, as they drifted back down from heaven in each other's arms. She told him tenderly, "You sure know how to treat a gal, Mr. Custer. I don't know why, but most men seem anxious to climb off and light out, once they've had their way with me. I don't mind saying that can leave a gal feeling mighty confused and hurt."

"Some less experienced gents must feel sort of shy, afterwards, I reckon."

She hugged him closer and murmured, "I wish *I* was a mite more experienced. I reckon you could tell I haven't done this as often as I might want. I've never managed to keep a regular boyfriend, for some reason, and the lovers a gal seems to meet up with in real life don't act at all like the lover boys in the romantical books I like to read. I get to *read* more about loving than I get to *do* it. But I reckon you don't find that too surprising, right?"

He caressed one of her breasts with his free hand and kissed the side of her throat as he told her reassuringly, "Most folk get to read more about life than they might want out of it. I can see how slinging hash in such a quiet neck of the woods might cut down on a gal's chances for real romance."

She sighed. "That's the pure truth. That last gent I even got to kiss was a windmill salesman who stopped here more than six or eight weeks ago, and he treated me sort of shabby. I can't remember ever having a lover as romantical as *you*. How come you like me so much, Mr. Custer?"

Longarm kissed her full on the lips to avoid having to answer as he pondered the matter for himself. But even as he congratulated himself on his charity, he couldn't seem to work up as much dismay about her looks as he knew he ought to. What they'd said about Cleopatra's nose or Boody Mary's waistline was the simple truth. The visible details that made up the differences between a homely woman and a head-turner just didn't *show* in the dark. Kitty's naked flesh was smooth, soft, and clean. Her responsive body was in good shape from honest toil, whatever shape it might have in a cheap waitress get-up. He recalled the color of her hair as somewhere between spiderweb and mouse. But unbound and spread out on his pillows it felt soft and thick as any other hair he could recall. As for how she felt where it really mattered, that reminded him so he moved one pillow down to thrust under her hips as she raised her knees and moaned, "Oh, *could* we, some more?"

They could and they did. And when she finally

protested she had to get back to her own room, he was sorry to see her go.

It just wasn't true that the Great White Father had no sense of humor, although said humor was perhaps a mite sardonic when it came to playing jokes on Mister Lo. For the Crow Agency set up in the wake of the real Mr. Custer's misadventure with the Lakota Confederacy was only a short hike, on foot, from where a third of the Seventh Cav lay buried atop Last Stand Ridge. The Lakota had won the battle, but the Crow had wound up with the battlefield.

The Crow had been rewarded with about ten thousand square miles of the land Red Cloud, Sitting Bull, Crazy Horse, and Gall had fought for, because the Crow had served as valuable allies—or traitors —during the so-called Sioux Wars, depending on who you were talking to. Back in the Shining Times of the Horse Indian the Crow had been the Sparrow Hawk clan of the Lakota or Sioux Nation. Fortunately for the spread of white civilization—for the Crow were tough as any other Lakota—they had some sort of religious argument with the main branch of their family, and it had resulted in the burning hatred only a family quarrel can generate. So, by the time the first whites had met *any* of them, the so-called Crow and so-called Sioux had been at it hammer and tongs for a spell. The outnumbered Crow had been getting the stuffing kicked out of them up until then. So, on the principle that He Who Fights My Enemy Must Be My Friend, the Crow had thrown in with the whites against their hated cousins.

It just wasn't true that the U.S. Army had been sent west to slaughter Indians in general. Crow, Pawnee, and Western Delaware had slaughtered many an Indian enemy for them. The Crow, in particular, had made valuable scouts against the Lakota, because in a pinch they could naturally *pass* for Lakota. They spoke the same lingo and used the same medicine. Issued army weapons and ammunition, they had probably killed as many Lakota in their time as the uniformed troops of the Great White Father. Both sides agreed that the Battle of Little Bighorn might have gone a whole lot different had Custer's Crow scouts, instead of Custer, been in command. For there wasn't a Lakota trick a Crow might not know, or top.

Knowing all this, Longarm wasn't as upset as some whites might have been when he got off the train just north of where Custer had died to find nobody in charge of the open platform, no sign of his saddle, and an old woman shouting curses at him from her unpainted frame cabin across the tracks. A couple of Indian kids came out of another B.I.A.-issue shack to sort of bark at him like dogs and throw dirt clods in his general direction. He knew they would have aimed better if they had really meant it.

He cradled his Winchester over an elbow and lit a cheroot as he stood his ground to see what happened next. What happened next was a couple of mean-looking youths on painted ponies.

They came dashing out of nowhere to ride in circles around him and the platform, shouting and whooping as if they took him for a wagon ring or perhaps a lone and done-for Lakota. Longarm thought the one pegging arrows at him was sort of overdoing it, but he knew he was supposed to dance when an arrow thudded into the planking inches from his boots, so he didn't. He just stared at them. Then an older Crow on an army bay rode in to yell something dreadful at them and they had to stop and ride off, laughing.

Longarm's rescuer was dressed semi-white in yellow-striped cavalry pants, a buckskin jacket, and a high-crowned black Stetson with an eagle feather stuck in its beaded band. He had a federal badge a lot like Longarm's pinned to his buckskin shirt. So Longarm wasn't surprised when the old-timer reined in to say, "I am called Laughing Raven. I am a sergeant in the Indian Police. If you are Longarm, we have your possibles over at the station house. If you are not Longarm, you had better tell me what you are doing here and what you want. This land, all this land, belongs to my nation alone."

The white lawman said, "I'm called Longarm. I wasn't sent to pester your people. I'm looking for one of my own people called Maxwell Windsor. I was told he was last seen here."

Laughing Raven nodded soberly. "He was. We know why you have come. Why is it that you people never listen to us? We told Custer *he* was going the wrong way, too. The crazy man who drew pictures wouldn't listen, either. Now he is lost in bad country to the southwest. You won't find him. Some of us have already looked. Come. You will want some ponies as well as the things you sent ahead last night."

Longarm nodded and followed as the Indian swung his mount around and headed for the more clustered part of the sort of spread-out settlement. Little kids stuck their tongues out at him from their dooryards as they passed, but now that it was official he was there, no adult Indians wanted to pay any attention to him. Longarm spotted a sun-faded flag flapping listlessly above the only house in town that had been whitewashed and asked if that was where their white agent lived.

Laughing Raven said, "Yes. But he and his woman are down in Garrytown today. There was a fight at the Garrytown trading post, so there has to be a trial. Before they left, our agent told us about you and said it would be a good thing if we helped you as much as we could. Hear me, we can feed you. We can give you ponies. You can't have any of our young women, and we don't *know* where that other fool went after he left here."

Longarm glanced up at the sun and replied, "The day is young. All I need is a fair start in the right direction. Did they leave here by way of some trail, or did they just dude off across the open grass?"

Laughing Raven said, "Both. After we get you mounted I will show you where we lost his trail. It is not far. He followed the wagon trace beyond the place where Custer fought. But his cart left no tracks as far as where Reno fought. It reads that somewhere along Greasy Grass Ridge they turned off the trail for some reason. One of my police trackers thinks they might have wanted to camp under the trees along the Little Bighorn. He found one of the little paint tubes the crazy man uses down near the water. I don't know why anyone would want to camp in such a place. Many Lakota died of their wounds, down among those trees, after the big fight. Aside from the spirits of unscalped enemies, it was a bad time of the year to camp in a draw. The Little Bighorn was over its banks. If a flash flood doesn't get you in the early green-up the mosquitoes and the black flies will."

By this time they had made it to a somewhat larger shack with bars across some of the windows and a pole corral full of ponies out back. Someone inside must have been watching. A younger Crow lawman came out packing Longarm's saddle and gear. For some fool reason, he was grinning like a mean little kid.

Laughing Raven didn't dismount. He told Longarm, "It might be best if you chose your own pony.

My young men mean well, but they seldom get the chance to see one of you people fall on his ass."

By this time three more Crow had come out to see the fun and a prisoner locked up inside was grinning wolfishly out at him through the bars. Longarm took his gear with a nod of thanks and carried it over to drape across a corral pole as they all tagged along. He told Laughing Raven, "I need at least two. Both should be fit to pack or ride. I mean to change mounts every few miles."

Laughing Raven nodded. "That is a good way to cover plenty of ground. You can have any two you choose."

Longarm dropped his cheroot, snuffed it out with his boot, and looked the remuda over a spell before he decided, "I like that bobtail buckskin and the brown and white paint."

Laughing Raven said something in his own sing-song lingo and one of the other Crow handed Longarm a braided leather throw-rope without comment. It wouldn't have been fair to say their manners were worse than most white cowhands' might have been in the same sort of situation. Rustic humor was about as subtle no matter where a stranger encountered it.

Longarm had been hazed the same way before. He just opened the gate, shook out a small show-off loop, and threw. He could tell from the admiring grunts behind him that the Indians were as surprised as he was when his first throw settled neatly on the buckskin before the half-wild animal could flinch out of the way. It was only after he had the son of a bitch roped that he began to suspect he might have picked the wrong pony.

The buckskin didn't want to come out of the corral, let alone be saddled and bridled. It had the weight and an extra set of hooves to dig in. But Longarm was big enough, when he threw in determination and horse savvy. So, playing the stubborn cuss something like a trout and something like a stump that had to be cleared one damned way or another, Longarm managed to work the buckskin out the gate and one Indian was gracious enough to swing it shut after them. But Longarm saw that was just to keep the other milling ponies inside. For, while by this time someone should have been helping him steady the buckskin, nobody was. He knew that they knew it was just plain impossible for one man to saddle and bridle a fighting pony. But, as they seemed content to let him try, he tried, and did it. It wasn't easy, and both Longarm and the buckskin were covered with dust and sweat by the time it was over. Even Laughing Raven was grinning and muttering in open admiration by the time Longarm was aboard the battered buckskin, shaking out another loop as he growled, "Somebody open that damn gate and let me at the paint."

Laughing Raven said, "Hear me, you are good. Where did you learn to mount an Indian pony from the right side? That is when most of your kind get kicked, bitten, or both."

Longarm smiled thinly. "A little Indian birdie told me. Might have been the same one as told *you* boys to always mount a stolen cavalry mount from the *left*. Horse are creatures of habit, no matter how they've been broken in. Now, about that other one I need . . ."

Laughing Raven shook his head and said, "My young men have had enough fun with you. You are a good rider, not an object of innocent laughter. That paint is not a good trail mount. Go get a packsaddle and plenty to eat at the trading post while my young men cut a decent pony out for you. I will wait here for you. You won't need a translator at the trading post."

44

Longarm nodded and spun the buckskin around to head for the flagpole in the near distance. He was beginning to get his bearings from his last visit here a year or so ago. The trading post was usually close to the agent's house, in any case.

The buckskin gave him a little more trouble when he dismounted out front. It didn't mind him getting off. It just didn't want to be tethered to the hitching rail. Longarm punched it in the muzzle and said, "We're going to get along a lot better if you cut this bullshit out, horse." Though the pony was accustomed to being spoken to in the Crow dialect, it seemed to get his message. He tethered it with a double hitch, anyway, and went on inside.

The licensed trader's wife was minding the post alone while he was away on business at another settlement. She was a motherly little woman who had been pretty before time's cruel teeth had wrinkled her up and rinsed all the color from her hair. When he told her who he was and where he was headed she produced a new pine packsaddle and said, "You'll need plenty of jerked beef. I can't recommend our pemmican to a Christian. They just don't make pemmican right these days. Without real buffalo fat and wild berries it tastes like mighty poor salami. You'll want extra flour for your coffee, of course, and . . . Oh, dear me, I keep forgetting it's *sugar* that we put in coffee. I get so used to grubbing our regular customers."

He said he took his coffee black and asked for canned beans and tomato preserves to eat cold on the trail. She seemed flustered and said she was sorry as anything, but that Indians didn't trust tin cans and wouldn't eat a tomato, canned or otherwise, at gunpoint. He said in that case he'd best pack along some extra jerky and flour. She made up for it by having plenty of chocolate, and cheroots even cheaper than

45

the brand he usually smoked. As she got the stuff out he sacked it and lashed it to the packsaddle on the counter between them. When they'd agreed it was a sensible load he asked her to total it up on paper and sign it for him. She looked sort of wistful and asked, "Oh, did you figure on us billing the government for it?"

He had, but as he noted how shabby the machine-lace collar of her faded print dress was, he shook his head. "No, ma'am. I mean to pay cash. But I'll need a receipt from you to get my money back from Uncle Sam."

She nodded, but blushed and lowered her eyes as she tried to come up with something better, but finally had to just plain tell him that she didn't know how to read or write. She added in a red-faced stammer, "I know all the numbers and I never cheat anybody. But my man handles all the bookkeeping and such. Maybe, did you write it up, I could manage my name, at least."

He smiled down at her. "That might not be lawsome, ma'am. But let's not worry about it. It ain't as if I just bought you out. What say I just pay you and we'll say no more about it?"

She said, "That's the way the Indians do it. Most of them can't read or write, neither. But how are you to get your money back, later?"

"I'll cheat on my expense account some other way. How come you're crying like that, ma'am?"

She dabbed at her old eyes as she sobbed, "I do so hate to look like a fool. I *did* start to school when I was little, back in Penn State, afore my elders moved west. But, somehow, there was always so many chores to tend that I just never got any more education. You must think I'm mighty country."

He took one of her work-worn hands in his. "I was riz sort of country, too, ma'am. I know all about

46

stopping school. For they held a War one time, when I was in my teens, and I was made to feel I was invited. Things happen that way to some of us. But anyone can see you're a lady of good family."

She brightened and said, "Why, I thank you, young sir. You may not believe this, but you're the *second* gent of quality who's calt me a lady this very year. Just this green-up a really fancy gent from back East allowed I looked so ladylike he wanted to up and draw my picture."

Longarm raised an eyebrow. "Could we be talking about a gent called Maxwell Windsor, ma'am?" She said they surely were, adding, "He gave me the picture he made of me as a present and left some other sketchings, as he calt 'em, with us for safekeeping. He said they'd get less beat-up, here at our post, and that he'd pick 'em up on his way back East. He was awfully nice, but just between you and me he wasn't a real artist. My husband agrees the poor man must have bad eyesight or a shaky hand. But, just the same, it was nice of him to *try* to paint my picture."

Longarm told her, "It might have been nicer than you thought if you own a signed original by Maxwell Windsor, ma'am. Would it be possible for me to see it?"

She said it would be possible for him to see *all* the stuff the artist had left with her. She led him into the back, where six or eight small canvases leaned, paint side to the wall, in a tiny storeroom. The old woman rummaged out the one the artist had done with her as his model and held it up, saying, "Here's the one he gave me as a present. My husband says it looks as if the gent was breaking in new brushes and had his paint mixed way too thick. But the *colors* are sort of nice, don't you think?"

Longarm couldn't make much sense of the gobbed-on chaos of too-bright colors at arm's length,

47

either. But he knew enough to tell the old woman, "He's a sort of tricky painter, ma'am. His stuff ain't meant to be looked at close. If that's really you, and not upside down, it would show from say ten or twenty feet away, see?"

She frowned. "Do tell? Well, this room ain't four feet across and I can't say much for the light. What if we was to take it out front and step back a ways?"

They did. The old woman still looked dubious as she leaned the portrait against a side wall in the sunlight. They both moved back through the dusty grass until, suddenly, as if a haze had cleared, they both saw how well the missing artist had captured her, wrinkles, twinkles, and all. The old woman gasped, clapped her hands together, and almost sobbed, "Oh, dear Lord, it's like a tintype, only better! You can't see the colors in tintype. Look, there was an oil lamp shining in my eyes when he painted me, fast as anything, and you can almost see the flame flickering in my eyes, and . . . How did he get it to look so *real*, except that I ain't really that nice-looking?"

Longarm said, "If I knew how to do that, I'd be a famous artist myself. He didn't flatter you, ma'am. He got you just the way you looked to him by lamplight."

She laughed like a young girl, told him to wait right there, and ran inside to fetch the other canvases she and her husband had dismissed as daubs. They soon had a modest art museum spread along the base of her side wall. As she saw what each one was really supposed to look like she kept laughing and saying she could hardly wait for her fool husband to get back. Two others were portraits of Indians, a man and a woman. The man was good-looking and seemed sort of smug about his bright red scalp roach that seemed to almost move in the breeze above his bear-greased black hair. The Indian gal in the other

48

picture was moon-faced and unhappy-looking. The remaining canvases were landscapes. Whatever the Eastern critics had said about some of Windsor's earlier tries, he had the rolling Montana prairie down pat, now. You could even tell he had painted at green-up time, when the short-grass was still winter-dead at the tips and coming up onion-shoot green at the roots. He even had the *dirt* the right color for moist prairie loam.

Some Indians, attracted by the novelty, had edged in to join Longarm and the old woman. One who spoke English laughed and opined, "Wa, that is young Iron Foot, costumed for the hawk dance we held during the first warm days, and that is just how Baskets Are Full looked when she was getting over the sickness she suffered last winter! I did not know the box you people use to make pictures could make them so *big,* with all the *colors.*"

Another Crow wearing the badge of the Indian Police joined them to tell Longarm, "The agent has some pictures like that. The crazy man stayed in their house a week or more and made a picture of the agent's woman. Laughing Raven sent me to tell you it is getting late. We have your pack pony ready, and he wants to know if you want to leave now."

Longarm said he was ready as he'd ever be and headed for the trading-post door to gather up his packsaddle and supplies. The old woman stopped him to ask, "Is it true what you said about that picture of me being worth real money?"

Longarm assured her that Maxwell Windsor's paintings sold for a pretty penny, but added that he couldn't put an exact figure on her treasure. She smiled sweetly and said, "Oh, I never mean to part with it. I just wanted to be able to tell my husband how wrong he was. That Mr. Windsor must be a genius as well as mighty nice. I surely hope nothing bad has happened to him."

Longarm said, "I know what you mean. I'll be mighty vexed if I can't bring him back safe and well. I can't do that unless I start looking for him, though. So I'd best get cracking."

Chapter 5

Longarm hadn't followed Laughing Raven far along the two-rut wagon trace to Garrytown, leading his still somewhat balky pack pony, before they came to the rise where a third of the Seventh Cav of '76 lay buried under scattered white headstones, each trooper buried about where he'd fallen. To his right, as they followed the bare windswept ridges, the shallow Little Bighorn rippled unseen through its timbered draw, for the cottonwoods and such were in full summer leaf, now.

Laughing Raven pointed at a larger headstone and told him, "That was where we found Yellow Hair. But his wives cried so much the army took his body east to bury at a place called West Point. I was scouting with the main column. That is why I am still alive. It was three or four days before we came to this place and saw what those Lakota had done. yellow Hair lay on his side, naked, with a bullet through his chest and another through his skull. I think he must have been dead when the man who took his hair shot him in the head to make sure."

Longarm raised an eyebrow. "Do tell? The official

version has it that they respected Custer too much to lift his hair or mutilate him."

Laughing Raven snorted in derision. "I told you his wives made a big fuss, and by the time they got his body back East, they would have had to seal it in lead sheathing, even if that polite story was true. I don't think the Lakota knew who they'd killed up here until they read it in the newspapers. It was not a good move. You people had been playing games with the Lakota until the fight got serious. Less than two summers after the big fight here, the Lakota Confederacy had been smashed and scattered to reservations far apart."

They rode on in silence for a time as Longarm tried to put the events of that earlier June day together. He'd been along this ridge before. He still couldn't figure how Custer's third of the Seventh had wound up so scattered as well as scalped. He knew that just a few miles south Major Reno and Captain Benteen had gone by the book and survived.

As if he had been thinking along the same lines, Laughing Raven told him, "The rise we're coming to, now, is called the Greasy Grass because the grazing there is better than anywhere else around here. Some say that is where the fighting started. I did not see it. I know that from Greasy Grass the blue sleeves scattered. It must have been a crazy fight. Some blue sleeves wound up in a wash, over that way, to die alone. Others, if one can believe the lying Lakota, charged down the slope into the camp itself. Most wound up with Yellow Hair on Last Stand Ridge, back there. I think the officers must have been hit in the first confusion. I knew Captain Keough, who fought here. He was not a fool. Yellow Hair had fought Indians before, too. Wa, I think the dog soldiers guarding the big encampment down there among the trees must have opened fire on sight, and naturally they would have aimed at the officers first."

Longarm stared soberly down into the timbered draw again as he mused aloud, "From up here, the troopers couldn't have been able to count lodges worth a damn. Scouting out ahead on Terry's orders, poor old Custer likely thought he was riding against the usual war band of thirty or forty lodges and, yeah, the rules he thought he was still playing by called for Mister Lo to *run* from close to three hundred troopers, not *attack* 'em."

Laughing Raven grimaced. "We *told* Terry the enemy was gathering here in big numbers. We had Crow pretending to *be* damned Lakota. We told Terry the Cheyenne, Blackfoot, and even some Arapaho from the south were coming to join the hostiles that summer. But you people never listen."

By this time they were on the rise called Greasy Grass. The Crow reined in, pointed at a clump of soapweed, and added, "That crazy man who paints with too many colors would not listen to us, either. This is where they turned off the trail with the cart. They went down the slope into the trees. That is all we know. I would help you scout for sign down there. I have no fear of spirits in the daytime. But, as I told you, my young men lost their trail down by the water many weeks ago. You will find nothing, nothing, this late in the summer. The river has been over its banks more than once since they camped down there."

Longarm fished out a cheroot and lit up before he opined, "I can't see even a greenhorn making camp so soon after leaving your agency back there. You say one of your boys found an empty paint tube. Try it this way. Say the artist wanted to make a study of the old camp ground. We know he works fast. Even if he painted more than one fool tree it wouldn't have

53

taken him more than an hour or so. Then they'd have forded the river and headed on west for the regular Bighorn, right?"

Laughing Raven shrugged and answered, "If you say so. That is not the way *I'd* try to get there. The regular trails through the Bighorn Range run well north or south of here."

Longarm nodded, but said, "Mayhaps his breed guide knew some short-cut through the hills. Would you know what nation half of him hails from?"

Laughing Raven shook his head. "I only spoke with him once or twice, in English. He did not speak our tongue. So he is neither part Crow nor part Lakota. I don't think he was Cheyenne, either. Cheyenne are good enemies. They look a man in the eye when they talk to him. The boy the crazy man hired was that camp-dog kind of breed neither your people nor mine think much of. Hear me, there are good men, *good,* of mixed blood. I never fought Comanche, but they say Quanna Parker is all man. I think that guide—they call him Johnny Two Hats—must be trash white and begging Indian. I did not like him. I would not trust him to lead me to the trading post. It's no wonder the people you are searching for seem to be lost."

Longarm said, "Well, they sure ain't up *here.* I thank you for leading me this far, and now I'd best see where old Johnny Two Hats might have led poor Maxwell Windsor."

He jerked the lead line to get his black pack pony's nose up out of the greasy grass and headed down the slope as his Crow guide turned homeward without comment, at a lope. Longarm knew tall timber tended to make nomadic plains dwellers a mite uneasy, even when it wasn't said to be haunted. So just how good a job the Crow had done down by the river was still to be determined.

As he rode into the trees along the river, he found the deep shade a mite spooky, himself. Some of the trees were even oak and none had ever been cut for firewood. Longarm had met old Tatanka Yatanka, better known as Sitting Bull. So he wasn't surprised the wily Pope of the Hunkpapa Teton Lakota had chosen such a site for his big pow-wow. Sitting Bull hadn't wanted to make it easy to judge the size of the encampment from any distance. He had no doubt had to reassure some of the gathered Indians about the spirits he knew so well, too. Even in late June the damned draw would have been buggy and snake-infested.

Neither of Longarm's Indian ponies liked it all that much this summer, from the way they were spooking at shadows. Longarm knew critters could sense things better than humans. So he felt a mite spooked, himself, as he reined in to peer about in the gloom. There was a brooding silence among the trees. There should have been more birds. He saw no traces left by the long-gone Indians. There wasn't much grass growing in the heavy shade, but the ground was scoured by flood water where it wasn't covered with leaf litter. The Indians had pulled out four or five spring floodings ago. Yet there was still a lingering hint of death in the air. Longarm held his cheroot well clear of his nose as he studied on that with a few thoughtful sniffs. He just couldn't tell whether his imagination was remembering all the wounded Indians who must have died down here among the trees, or whether he was really inhaling the faint fumes of an old battle ground. He couldn't smell anything *really* stinky. The soil was likely a mite sour from the constant damp shade.

He rode on. Closer to the banks of the now-low Little Bighorn he spotted something shining dully near what looked like a bit of busted-up furniture.

He dismounted and hunkered down for a better look. The paint tube was easy to figure. It had been filled with zinc white oil paint before it had been flattened total and empty. The stick near it looked like it had been busted off something. Not any red river cart. The slender length of hardwood was planed too smooth and varnished too fancy. He decided it had to be part of an artist's easel. He nodded and muttered, "He set up here to paint a mighty gloomy scene. Ran out of zinc white and managed to damage his easel getting it set up after clumsy packing in that bitty crowded cart."

As he rose he spotted the stub of a cottonwood branch someone had helped himself to with a knife and felt sort of pleased with himself. "Yep, this was where he repaired his busted easel, sure as hell. Now, where did they go from *here?*"

He remounted and rode down the bank to let his ponies water themselves in the fetlock-deep river as he got his bearings on his mental map of these parts.

As one moved west along the Montana–Wyoming line, he came in turn to progressively wetter rivers running more or less in line to join the Yellowstone to the north. Only the Yellowstone would qualify as a river back East, where rivers ran more serious. The Powder River was a mile-wide-and-inch-deep joke. The Tongue River west of the Powder ran a little wetter, and then this Little Bighorn ran wetter yet. Like the other prairie-fed streams to the east, the Little Bighorn ran deep or shallow according to how recently it had rained on the High Plains. But it got a little snowmelt, early in the year, from the Bighorn Range, which divided its watershed with the more serious Bighorn it got to join just before they both got lost in the Yellowstone. Maxwell Windsor had written home that he was bound for the basin of the

Bighorn, period. Was it possible the dude had meant the *Little* Bighorn?

Longarm blew cheroot smoke out his nose and growled, "I wish we hadn't thought of that. They did say *basin,* damn it, and this glorified creek don't have much of a basin. Come on, horses, let's keep heading west."

They did. They were soon out of the trees and heading up the far open rises toward the Bighorn Range. This close to where the Little Bighorn joined the Bighorn, they were only about ten miles away. From the top of any rise on the rolling prairie they looked a heap closer. They were way lower than the front ranges of the Rockies that formed the far wall of the Bighorn Basin, but they were imposing enough to qualify as real mountains back in West-By-God-Virginia. While there was no snow left on the peaks this late in the year, they were timber-covered as the Black Hills the Indians had been so fond of. He knew they'd *really* admired the complex *edges* where timberlands and grasslands met. For nothing beat such country for hunting. In their Shining Times, the horse Indians had left the deeper woods to the good and bad spirits and enjoyed the deer and elk that haunted the edges. The price Red Cloud had put on the Black Hills might not have been so steep had not the whites shot off the plains buffalo with such enthusiasm. The hills ahead were well inside this Crow reserve line. So any hunters he met up ahead figured to be more or less friendly Crow. He hoped any he might meet would give him a chance to explain he was a friendly white lawman and not a poacher after their elk skins.

Longarm got along better than most with Indians because he tried to see things the way they might look from Indian eyes. So, while he knew he was crossing Crow land with permission from both the

B.I.A. and the Indian Police, he kept a sharper look-out than a less experienced High Plains rider might have. Thus, it wasn't too long before he noticed he was being ghosted.

The first time he spotted the two riders tagging along after him, he reined in on a rise to wait for them, assuming they might be messengers from the agency he had just left. But they vanished below the skyline and stayed put while he finished a whole fresh smoke. So he lit another and decided, "Kids playing cowboys and Indians, I hope," and rode on.

A couple of hours later he was in the aspen and lodgepole pine of the Bighorn Range. He tethered his ponies upslope and eased back down a hundred yards with his Winchester to see what they might have to say for themselves.

It didn't work. He lay in ambush behind a fallen log for the better part of an hour and all he saw or heard was a redwing fussing at him about its nest in a nearby clump of wild cherry.

He finally said, "I'm sorry I bothered you, bird. If they was playful Crow kids they likely turned home to eat supper. If they're someone more serious, they're just too smart to crowd a man in tall timber. Meanwhile, this is no damn way to cross high country before dark."

He rose, worked his way back up to his ponies, and changed saddles to ride the black mare before moving on. She didn't seem to like it much, and a pony bucking amid trees had a sort of unfair advantage. So, after she'd tried to scrape his knees off a few times, he dismounted, got a cruel grip on her muzzle, and gently explained, "Your kind can't breathe through the mouth worth a hang. So, as you may have noticed, it's easy enough for little old me to suffocate you if you don't want to be my friend."

The pony tried to break free by twisting her head

considerably. But Longarm was big and strong in his own right, and since it soon sank in that he could kill her if he really wanted to, the black pony would have smiled sweetly at him, if she could, by the time he decided she'd had enough and let her breathe again. He said, "I hope we understand one another better now. For I ain't got time for bucking contests, even if you had money to bet. I'm going to mount you some more, now, and if you try to run any more pine needles through my hair, I'm likely to get mad as hell, hear?"

She seemed to understand. She gave him no further trouble as the three of them threaded on up the slope. There was no trail to follow. They made their own as they drifted back and forth, as the steepness of the slopes and outcrops of rock might indicate. It didn't take long to reach the top, that far north, and as he'd expected, a game trail ran north to south along the spine of the range. He turned south along it, explaining to his ponies, "I kind of like to stay with cover when folk I don't know might be dogging me. I know the crests get higher and steeper to the south, and I know it'll be sort of cold up here in a spell. But let's at least work our way off the reservation before we mosey down to the open basin to the west."

The range was timbered to the top, and he couldn't get a good view of the open plains to either side. Since he and his ponies were as invisible to anyone else, within say a quarter mile it evened out. Some of the going got tough indeed as the game trail wound among massive outcrops or through sticker-bush only an elk or a grizzly would want to poke about in as a rule. Longarm could only judge their mileage by his pocketwatch and the way the afternoon sun slanted through the treetops all around. By the time the light was starting to get sort of tricky, he figured they were a twenty-mile crow-flight from the Crow Agency. He chose a grassy hollow to rein and announced, "This is where we'd best stop for the night, horses. It's as good a camp site as anyone but an eagle is likely to find up here before dark."

He dismounted, tethered the ponies side by side, and rubbed them both down as soon as he unsaddled them. He knew it would get a lot colder up here before it got warmer. Then he broke out the feed bags and watered them, a whole canteen's worth in each bag, before he served each a double handful of parched corn and told them, "There's plenty of grass in case you're more spoiled than most Indian ponies."

It was only after he had removed their nose bags and rubbed them down again that he was ready to deal with his own dubious comforts. He put on his sheepskins, unrolled his bedding, and sat on the same to warm it some with his rump as he ate dry jerky washed down with canteen water and a little medicinal Maryland rye. More refined cuisine would have called for a fire, and he just didn't know how alone he was up here this particular evening.

He studied on that as he enjoyed an after-supper smoke. He had paused more than once on the far side of the stickerbush, working this far south along the ridge, and that hadn't worked, either. Long-gone Indian kids seemed as likely as anyone else on his trail. That shootout in Sheridan could have been something left over from another case. A man made a lot of enemies riding for Uncle Sam, as he'd tried to tell Kim Stover that time she got all misty-eyed at him. An old grudge made more sense than someone trying to stop him from finding a lost greenhorn. For, if somebody else didn't want Maxwell Windsor found, they'd have to know why he was missing, and if they had anything to do with that, what in thunder could they be so worried about? A crook who couldn't hide a body or more in such a vast search area had to be dumb as hell. But, on the other hand, dumb crooks had come closer to killing Longarm in the past than most other kinds. Smart crooks tended to put as much distance as they could between themselves and a lawman of Longarm's reputation. It had mostly been the idiots who had chosen to shoot it out with him.

He blew a thoughtful smoke ring and muttered, "Or smart ones we had cornered. Sneaks who feared we was about to get *on* to 'em. But what in thunder could anyone be afraid I'll find that would make it worth the risk of gunning me to keep me from finding it? Dead or alive, that artist won't be able to tell me one thing *he* don't already know and, since he's an honest man, he'd have already told the law if he knew about anything unseemly going on in these parts. He never voiced any suspicions to the Indian Agent or Laughing Raven back there, and he spent plenty of time with 'em. He never wrote *home* about anything suspicious, or the friends and relations who want him found would have told us. All anyone *honest* knows is that he headed out this way to paint innocent landscapes and ain't been heard from since. It sure is a thundering puzzle."

It was getting cold as well as darker, now. Longarm snubbed his last smoke for the evening and got under the covers. He hung his hat and gun-rig over the swells of the saddle he was using for a pillow. He took the Winchester to bed with him, duds and all. He knew he'd sleep warmer as well as better if he shucked his outer duds and boots, but he was on the prod and meant to roll out ready for war if he had to.

Somewhere in the night an owl bird hooted. But it

had done so farther along the ridge rather than from back the way he'd just come and, what the hell, the Indians said an owlhoot didn't count unless it seemed to be calling you by name.

Chapter 6

By nine the next morning, Longarm and his ponies had made it out of the timber on the far side of the range and were fording the Bighorn, where it hugged the foothills to get around them and join its baby brother on its way to the bigger Yellowstone. The grass on either side was getting summer-brown by now, but there was still enough water in the riverbed to make a rider worry about quicksand. They didn't run into any. The Bighorn just tried to discourage then by running stirrup-deep in places. Because it was a more serious river, it didn't allow as much timber along its banks. There was some willow and young cottonwood, of course, but every few years the Bighorn roared through these parts deep and mean enough to uproot factory chimneys. That was why the western line of the Burlington left the otherwise handy basin far upstream at its junction with the Shoshoni.

Once across, Longarm found the wagon trace *cum* cattle trail he had expected, running more or less along the north-south flood plain of the river. One wagon rut looked much like any other, and it had been a good six weeks since the Windsor party had passed this way. But if they hadn't passed this way, that young breed who was guiding them had started out lost to begin with. There was just no better way to work south through the basin.

From time to time, Longarm reined in to look back as well as around. He saw a few scenes an artist might have thought worth painting. The purple mountains to both sides contrasted mighty nicely with the tawny buffalo grass between. But Longarm was really more interested in human figures forming part of the composition. He didn't see any. If anyone was still ghosting him, they had learned to hang well back.

He figured he was sixty miles or more from the Crow Agency when he topped a rise and spotted the rooftops of a trail town ahead. It took him another hour to ride into the little town of Hillsboro, population 300 when the herd was not in town.

Since he'd ridden in from Indian country *without* a herd, he attracted a certain amount of polite albeit intense interest when he tied up in front of the one saloon near the post office to see if they served decent draft beer or anything else he might be able to use. He'd no sooner bellied up to the bar and found the beer acceptable when the town law, two of them, joined him to wait politely for his expected words of explanation. The atmosphere improved when he casually spread his badge out on the mahogany. The senior Hillsboro peace officer said, "We've heard good things about you, Longarm. Didn't you smoke up the Shoshoni pretty good for us when they riz a few years back?"

Longarm nodded and modestly allowed the army had borrowed him from Justice that unsettling summer just to the southwest. Then he said, "I ain't scouting Indians this summer, boys. You'll never guess what a fool's errand they got me on this time."

The younger lawman said, "Sure we can. We got us a Western Union, just the same as everyone else. You're looking for that lost, strayed, or stolen artistic gent, Max something or other. Right?"

"Close enough. I don't reckon he might have passed through here?" Longarm asked.

The older peace officer answered, "Wrong. I had a drink with him right about here, maybe a month or more ago. That was afore we knowed he was lost, of course. He didn't let on he was lost when he come through here with a breed, a colored boy, and a red river cart. We just started getting wires about him in the past few days."

The other lawman said, "They stayed here overnight. Hired rooms at the hotel next door. All but the colored one, I mean. He had to bunk in the cart, of course. But he was all right. Sort of high-toned and polite for a nigger, as a matter of fact. The artist gent was even nicer. Stood a round of drinks right here where we're standing. And they say he gave a painting to the lady as runs the hotel."

Longarm nodded thoughtfully. "He sure parts with his stuff easy, considering what it's worth on the hoof. Did they say where they was headed after here?"

The older lawman nodded. "I asked. Mr. Windsor said they was following the river south into Wyoming Territory. I warned him the Gray Bull was still in flood and that Fifteen Mile Creek was quicksandy even when it wasn't. But he said he had a good guide and meant to be caresome in any case."

Longarm asked what impression Johnny Two Hats had made in Hillsboro. They both seemed to hesitate before the older one decided, "Hell, there's no sense standing on ceremony with a fellow peace officer.

The boy was a breed saddle-tramp, if you want to compliment him some. He said his daddy had been a mountain man and that his mammy had been an Indian princess. That's a mighty fancy title for a digger squaw, if you ask me."

Longarm asked, "How did you figure his Indian blood as Ho?"

The old-timer told him, "Because when pressed he told one of the boys he was part Shoshoni, which was a lot of bull. For he rid like a greenhorn, not a man who was even part Horse Indian. He said he knew this country. That was bull, too. For he thought the rail town of Lovell was over a day's ride south along the river, when it's really only about twenty miles and not on the river at all."

The younger lawman said, "That's right. Lovell's a good ten miles west of the Bighorn, on the Shoshoni. You'd surely expect a *Shoshoni* to know that, considering how that river got its name. They used to come down it regular to fight the Crow in the Shining Times. Paiutes and other diggers talk the same lingo as Shoshoni, Ute, and other real Indians. I reckon if *I* was part digger I'd be ashamed to say so, too."

Longarm inhaled some more suds and said, "An Indian I just met had a poor opinion of Johnny Two Hats as well. But the point is that they got *this* far with no trouble. Since that other town's so close, I can make it easy by this afternoon and see what they have to say about the party there."

The older lawman shook his head. "No, you can't. We just told you we got a Western Union, and so has Lovell. Unless the town law down there is a big fibber—and I hope he ain't, because my sister married him—your Maxwell Windsor never made it that far south. Nobody in Lovell ever seen hide nor hair of him, his hands, or his cart."

Longarm frowned. "Well, that does narrow it

down some, if he vanished between here and a town only twenty miles away, with open range to lose his fool self in."

But the old-timer shook his head and said, "We've already looked. So have riders out of Lovell. You're right about it being open country. There's just no place one could hide three men, four ponies, and a red river cart between here and there. We've come to the considered opinion that they never got to Lovell because, like the boy here says, they missed it entire by following the river and the advice of that fool breed. You can ride right past Lovell, easy, if you don't know it's ten miles up a side stream. The next town smack on the river would be Basin, Wyoming, and afore you ask, nobody in Basin ever saw hide nor hair of 'em, neither."

The younger lawman said, "To reach Basin they'd have had to cross the Gray Bull, in flood. What say they got swept away instead of across? Did the Bighorn carry 'em past here, all busted up, at night, nobody here would have noticed. If you ask me, the best place to look for them greenhorns right now would be up along the Yellowstone. Something might have wound up on a sandbar. Otherwise, with six weeks to drift, under muddy water, they could be anywhere betwixt here and the Gulf of Mexico by now!"

Longarm wanted to object. But unfortunately the youth's grim notion worked as well as a red river cart vanishing into thin air on open range. Longarm finished his schooner and told them he meant to have a word with the hotel lady next door before he headed on up the Bighorn.

As he left the younger one assured him, joyfully, that he was wasting his time. Longarm didn't argue. The kid could be all too right. But Billy Vail had ordered him to search for Windsor in the Bighorn Basin, not New Orleans.

The hotel was more like a fair-sized frame house with a few rooms to let upstairs. But the place smelled clean and the lady who ran it was a handsome young widow woman in a freshly laundered print mother hubbard and neither powder nor paint. She likely knew she didn't need it. She was still too young for the dry Montana winds to have messed up enough to matter, although her chestnut hair was a mite sun-bleached here and there. It was naturally pinned up properly for this time of day and her perfume smelled more like a daylit garden than evening primrose. She said they called her Sandra Grant and that she remembered Mr. Windsor fondly. She asked Longarm if he would like to see the real oil painting the artist had given her. When he nodded she led him back to her own quarters, where the unframed canvas was mounted above her stone fireplace. She told him, "You have to stand back to see how good it is. He paints with a butter knife, I think. They calls that sort of painting 'impressed.' "

Longarm gave her credit for having a good eye for art as well as household dust. The oil sketch was a landscape. The country looked familiar, but Longarm had been viewing a lot of country lately. He told her how much he admired her present and asked, "While they was here, did you get any impression Windsor had anything bothering him?"

She gasped and said, "Oh, pooh! Impression, that was the word, not impressed. He seemed sort of jolly, as a matter of fact. I can't say I thought much of that part-Indian boy he had with him, although, to be fair, the boy didn't do anything wrong while they stayed here. I counted the silver the moment they left, to make sure. But, I don't know, had it been up to me I'd have rather let a room to that colored man instead of the breed. He was much more polite and, if you ask me, I suspect he was wearing cleaner underwear."

Longarm didn't ask why, in that case, she had had to refuse service to Windsor's colored valet. He knew the valet was used to being kept in his so-called place even if the War had been said to settle such matters over a dozen years ago. He thanked her for her time and courtesy, to him, and asked if she served board as well as room.

She gave a little shrug and said, "I feed guests when I *have* any. This is our slow season. I don't think we've had a dozen guests since that nice Mr. Windsor was here. Why do you ask?"

He answered, truthfully, that it wasn't important. He knew he could pick up some canned cow-camp grub at the local general store before he rode on. It saved him shaving for a sit-down noonday dinner, in any case.

He ticked his hat brim to her out front and turned to leg it across the one street toward the general store next to the smithy, which just about covered the business opportunities of Hillsboro that summer. The sun was high and beginning to make itself felt by now. Longarm was still wearing the sheepskins. So he'd just quickened his step to make the shade on the far side when all hell commenced to bust loose at once.

He heard Miss Sandra scream and a gun going off just about the time a mighty noisy bumblebee seemed to grab his hat and run off with it. By this time he had, of course, taken a running dive over the watering trough in front of the smithy to land on one shoulder and keep rolling into the dark, smoky depths, to scare hell out of the older gent working at the anvil. As he rolled to his own feet, sixgun in hand, he told the smith, "Get to some cover, and I thank you for not having no horse in my way just now."

He didn't see anything out front, but the deserted street still echoed to the sound of more than four shots. Anyone could count three shots without counting. After that it was four or more. A distant voice called out, "Longarm?" and he called back, "I hear you. What's your pleasure, you . . . Never mind. Ladies present."

A familiar figure exposed himself in the gap between the saloon and Miss Sandra's place. Since it was the young lawman he had just been jawing with in the saloon, Longarm moved out, still keeping his own gun trained that way, as he demanded, "What's up over there?"

The younger man called back, "He ain't up. He's down. I seen him throw down on you just now, so I done what I had to."

Longarm didn't holster his own gun until he was halfway across and could see the denim-clad shoulders, exposed fists, and hatless head of the man at the town law's feet. By the time Longarm reached them the older lawman had joined his son, deputy, or whatever, and Miss Sandra was staring over her picket fence at him, muttering, "Oh, dear, I'd best get some hot water and clean linen."

The boy who'd shot the stranger in the back shook his head and said, "He don't need no medical attention, Miss Sandra." Then he turned to the older lawman and added in a desperately casual voice, "I never had time to call him, Dad. It was backshoot him or let him backshoot Longarm, here."

The older lawman said, "You done right, boy. Where in the U.S. Constitution do it say a backshooter deserves a call?"

The youth shrugged and replied, "I still would

70

have like it better had I took my first man fair and square."

Longarm said, "No, you wouldn't have. But all that will come to you later. Are you certain this gent on the ground was a lone wolf? My reason for asking is that I thought I had two riders ghosting me, about this time yesterday."

The youth shook his head. "I didn't see anyone else. I didn't even see how he rid in *alone!* I was on my way to the . . . going out back, when I spied him slipping betwixt the buildings from ahint and tagged after him to see what he might be up to. What he was up to only got obvious a split second afore I had to gun him. I *would* have called him, durn it, but he already had his gun out and,—"

"Aimed good," Longarm cut in. "He'd have blowed my poor unsuspecting head off had not I moved unexpected just as he fired. Remember that if you ever have to gun anyone from that range. Head-shooting is tricky, even from up close. I see you done him right, though, smack in the small of the spine."

Sandra looked sort of sick and turned away to run into her place. The older lawman hunkered down to roll the dead man over. All three of them gasped when they got their first good look at his face. But Longarm wasn't really sure until the old-timer muttered, "Johnny Two Hats, sure as hell. But if he's supposed to be guiding Maxwell Windsor, how come he seems to be in town alone, trying to gun *you?*"

Chapter 7

Considering the short notice she had had, Sandra Grant managed to cook a mighty fine dinner by the time Longarm had finished his chores at the livery stable, Western Union, and such. When he had told her he would be staying at her hotel at least one night after all, he had hoped, at best, for early afternoon ham and eggs. But when he got back to her she had somehow managed steak and mashed potatoes with gravy. She wanted to serve his dinner in her dining room until he told her he could hardly ask a lady to waste a dining-room clean-up on one guest. So she sat him at her kitchen table near the screen door and had some coffee, herself, across from him.

Like most folk reared country, Longarm tended to take in his grub without much dinner-table conversation. But being a woman and only having one cup and saucer to manage, the pretty young widow woman kept jawing at him as he ate. He didn't mind. She had a pleasant voice and she seemed to be on his side.

"I can't say I'm not pleased to have a guest during our slow season," she said. "But it hardly seems fair

73

of them to keep you here in Hillsboro until they've held the hearing on that dead breed. Nobody in town has pressed charges and, even if they had, it was Junior Briggs who gunned him."

Longarm washed some spuds down with coffee to give himself time to think as well as a way to answer. He'd been sending so many names hither and yon by wire that it took him a moment to recall that the older town law was Big Joe Briggs, while his son and chief deputy was Junior. There was yet another younger brother serving as assistant deputy. Longarm hadn't met him yet. The Briggs clan was intermarried with the law from Lovell. Local elections likely resembled family get-togethers.

He told his landlady, "They ain't holding me here unfair, Miss Sandra. Aside from owing a fellow lawman who just saved my life the common courtesy of appearing before the coroner's jury for him, we've all put our heads together to see if we can slicker someone who's been acting slick and sneaky. They wanted to get up a posse and ride out in every direction after nobody they might know on sight until I talked 'em out of it just now."

She said, "I heard some of the argument, out front, as I was firing up my range. Maybe it's because I'm just a girl, but I got the impression Junior Briggs *got* the murderous breed just now."

Longarm shook his head. "This is a small town surrounded by open range. Johnny Two Hats didn't leave a pony tethered out front or out back. So he must have walked in, or crept in, sneaky, whilst his sidekick held his pony ready for his getaway in some nearby draw. That's who we're after, now. For, if only we can take him alive . . ."

"How do you know there were two of them?" she asked.

"Two riders was following me. That's how they

74

knew I was here in Hillsboro. It had to be somebody watching me ride in and not ride out. Nobody could have been set up here to wait for me, because I didn't know I was coming my own self. They did have the Crow Agency staked out, because someone aside from my boss found out what my orders was. All sorts of folk could have heard I was on my way to search for that lost artist by the time the B.I.A. sent for me."

He swallowed some steak and coffee before he continued, "I suspicion I'm dealing with a mighty cowardly master-mind who sends in the dumb and ugly to deal me out of the game, whatever the game might be. The two who followed me all the way from the Crow Agency didn't have the nerve to close in on me in open country, knowing it was two of them against a Winchester and, in all modesty, a man who knows how to aim pretty good. After I'd been here in town a spell, the one I suspect was in command sent his otherwise useless young breed in to see if he could get the drop on me, dark-alley style. He did. But thanks to old Junior Briggs, the yellow-belly waiting outside town was left mortified with two ponies and no doubt an urgent desire to be somewhere else as sudden as he could get there."

"But you wouldn't let Marshal Briggs go after him with a posse?" she objected.

"That's what he'd expect. Right now he's no doubt riding scared, looking back a lot, as he tries to throw a bunch of riders off his trail. It wouldn't be too tough a chore with the sod baked summer-hard, away from the river, and many a timbered draw to duck in and out of. I figure he'll hang on to the spare mount. Aside from its value, he wouldn't want a strange stray pony giving us a line on the general direction he lit out in. He'll put plenty of distance between himself and Hillsboro before he risks showing himself on any skyline again. But in time he'll figure he got away, and that's when we'll get the chance to get him."

She looked sincerely puzzled, so he added, "I told Big Joe Briggs not to send out any riders from here, with or without a second pony in tow. Meanwhile, we wired Aberdeen to the north, Lovell to the south, and Warren to the west to keep an eye peeled for strangers making for the railroad line in the company of an extra pony packing a riding saddle, not a pack-saddle."

She dimpled. "My, that was smart of you! But what if he's not headed for the railroad line, Custis?"

"We won't catch him. It still beats letting a mess of cowhands chase off in every direction to confuse things even more. If he's scared—and he ought to be—he'll want to catch a train out of this basin as fast as he can. If he *ain't* that scared it means he's still after me. That could give me another chance at him."

She suppressed a shudder. "Don't you mean you'll be giving *him* another chance at *you?* He knows who you are and what you look like, even at a distance. You don't have any notion who he is, or even if he's a *he!* For all you know, that breed could have been traveling with a Shoshoni squaw!"

Longarm frowned thoughtfully. "Anything is possible. But I have it on Indian authority that Johnny Two Hats wasn't related to no local Indians. He was last seen in the company of a white man and a colored man. I'm supposed to be looking for the white man. I'll sure wind up surprised when and if I learn Maxwell Windsor is trying to bushwack me to keep me from finding him. By all accounts, Windsor's colored valet is an old employee and Eastern-bred to boot. I'm hoping, mighty hard, that the breed got fired or deserted the party. For, if that ain't what

76

happened, I might not find that artist or his valet alive."

She asked him if he would like some of her marble cake and when he said yes she rose to fetch it from her pantry. She was just cutting him a generous slice when the screen door opened to admit the town law. Sandra smiled and said, "Set yourself down and have some coffee and cake, Big Joe."

The marshal shook his head and told her, "I just et. Thanks just the same. I come to tell Longarm, here, a thundering wonder we just now got a wire about."

Longarm told him to fire away. Big Joe said, "The late Johnny Two Hats just got out of Sing Sing Prison, way back in New York State. He was born in Virginia City to a part-Paiute lady of ill repute and shocking habits. His paternity ain't that clear. Despite his name, he was riz more townee than Indian, and he drew five at hard for a robbery he pulled off a long way indeed from Virginia City, Nevada. You'll never guess where the bakery he tried to stick up might have been."

Longarm said, "It would have had to be in New York State. Sing Sing is a state prison."

Big Joe sighed. "Aw, you spoiled half my surprise. The other half is that New York State says he was running with a gang of Eastern toughs, the last time they looked. He must have come back out West mighty recent."

"As a hired sneak," Longarm growled. "Maxwell Windsor is a New Yorker. Knowing he was heading out here to paint, someone planted that treacherous Johnny Two Hats in his party."

"To do what?" Big Joe asked.

Longarm said, "I wish you hadn't asked that. I'm still working on it. It couldn't have been to lead him *too* far astray. We know the breed led him into the

Bighorn Basin. *This* far into it, at any rate. To murder him after he got him all the way out here would not be beyond a gent your boy just established as a would-be killer. But that makes no sense. Anyone back East who wanted the man dead would have found it a lot easier just to murder him *there* in the *first* place. Why go to all this trouble? And if the poor man *has* met with foul play, why are they so anxious to keep me from looking for him?"

Sandra decided, "Maybe someone is afraid you'll *find* him."

Longarm objected, "So far, I ain't, and if *I'd* done away with a man or more a good six weeks ago I'd have spent a lot more time trying to hide the results than to keep one man from *looking* for 'em. The ground was soft when last the party was seen. Joe Junior is right about the rivers in flood carrying many a secret clean out of these parts. In all modesty, it has to cost more to hire folk to go up against me than they'd charge for pick and shovel work. So, no matter how you slice it, they fear I'm likely to find something out that they just don't *want* found out."

Big Joe opined, "Since the party was last seen near here, and since my boy just shot one member of said party, I shall venture an educated guess that what they don't want you to find can't be too *far* from here, Longarm."

"Yeah, and, damn it—sorry, ma'am—since last anyone but Johnny Two Hats was seen alive, the sod in all directions has had plenty of time to heal and the soil's baked hard as a banker's heart."

The full moon seemed to be sitting on Longarm's windowsill like a big fat pumpkin as it bathed his hired room in its soft, romantic light. Longarm was glad. For, while there was much to be said for making love in the dark with homely gals, Sandra Grant was pretty as a picture, even with her duds on, and built like a Greek goddess in the nude. As they lay there sharing a smoke in the moonlight with the covers kicked over the foot of the fourposter, she asked for the third or fourth time, "You won't tell anyone, will you, Custis?"

He snuggled her closer to his bare chest. "I'd rather be famous as a fighter than a lover, little darling. What kind of a polecat would kiss and tell in a town this size, to begin with?"

"I still feel as if the whole town was watching when we got so wild just now. How did that happen, anyway? I would have said *no*, if you'd given me the chance to say *yes*. But all I remember is offering politely to light your way to bed, and then I was *in* it, and . . . Oh, Custis, how did you ever get me to do such naughty things? I never made love like *that* when my husband was alive!"

He shrugged. "I don't recall asking. If you just can't wait for the cold gray dawn to have cold-gray-dawn second thoughts, I ain't got you hogtied, you know."

She sighed and said, "I know all too well. It's always sounded so crude, but I reckon it's true what they say about another slice not seeming all that important once the loaf's been cut and, oh, Custis, it's been so long and you make me so hot!"

He stretched out his free arm to snuff the cheroot in the ashtray on the bed table as he grinned and said, "Well, seeing as we seem to have our second wind, now . . ."

But, as he rolled her over on her back and shoved a pillow under her trim hips, she covered her breasts with her arms and pleaded, "Can't we close the shutters, dear? I feel so . . . so *naked* with the moonlight so bright across this bed."

He got into position as he soothed, "You're *sup*-

79

posed to be naked to do this right, honey. It looks even dirtier when a gal has her socks and shimmy on in this position."

She laughed and then they went too deliciously crazy to talk for a spell. When she finally came to her senses again she stared down at him in wonder to ask, "How did I wind up on top and, ooh, I *felt* that, you horny thing. How many times do you think we've come so far?"

He pulled her bare breasts down against his chest and kissed her before he said, "If you've been keeping score, you ain't been enjoying it as much as me."

She giggled. "I just had to *ask* you, didn't I? I could swear you were still hard, down there, if I didn't know that was impossible."

"I'm still game if you are."

They were just getting good at it some more when some fool downstairs commenced to pound on the front door and yell Longarm's name. Sandra sat bolt upright atop him and covered her bare breasts again, sobbing, "Oh, Lord, my poor reputation!"

He told her not to be silly as he rolled her off and got up to stick his head out the window and call down, "Who's down there calling my name in vain at this infernal hour? I was just enjoying the sleep of the just, damn it!"

Junior Briggs called up, "My dad sent me to fetch you. We just got a wire from Warren, and you was right. He rid for the railroad."

Longarm called back, "Do tell? Keep your voice down, lest we wake Miss Sandra. I hope the law in Warren took the cuss alive?"

Junior replied in a softer wail, "Not exactly. He's still alive. But he shot his way clear. They know who he is, though. He's a Montana cow thief widely admired for his skill with a running iron as well as a gun. They calls him Scribe Henderson, and now they're even madder at him in Warren. For he winged two deputies and kilt one total, leaving town faster than he rid in. He left that extra pony by the depot. They say the one he's still riding moves fast."

"I'll be down as soon as I can locate my own gun-rig, Junior. Where's your dad and the others? Next door in the saloon?"

"For now they are. My dad figures you'll want to set up a reception committee, should Scribe Henderson be headed back this way."

Longarm thanked him and ducked back inside. Sandra was standing beside the bed, putting her mother hubbard back on. He moved to kiss her and say, "Hell, we had time for a quick one, but mayhaps we'd best save it for now, little darling. There's no way that hired gun could make it back here, soon, even if he has the nerve. But I'd best go down and calm everyone else a mite lest they pester us again."

She said, "If you tell them, in the saloon, I'll never speak to you again. I don't know what on earth came over me tonight, and I'm so ashamed."

"I don't see why," he said. "We couldn't have been the only ones screwing, in a town of three hundred souls. If you mean to lock yourself in and cry about it, leave the front door downstairs unlocked, at least. I won't be gone long."

For some reason that made her blubber up and run out of the room. He muttered, "Women," and got dressed, no doubt faster than he might have if she hadn't.

Downstairs, he found the saloon sort of crowded and had to shake with hands who'd ridden in from outlying spreads to get in on the action which, so far, consisted of a lot of drinking at the bar and a game of stud someone had naturally started at a corner table. Marshal Briggs and his younger deputy son, Billy, were among the more serious-minded gents bellied up to the bar. Longarm ordered a needled beer and asked what all the fuss was about.

Big Joe said, "I thought it was obvious. Scribe Henderson is a killer, and he's after *you*, Longarm!"

The younger but more experienced lawman sipped some suds and said, "Not hardly. He didn't have the balls to come into town after me with Johnny Two Hats. He was trying to get *away*, not get *me*, when they spotted him and that extra pony way off in Warren this evening. By the way, have any extra details about that fight come in?"

Big Joe shook his head and replied, "Just that now he's got a real posse right on his tail and could be headed back this way. He's just established he knows how to kill, if he has to, and what if he's the mastermind you spoke about afore?"

Longarm said flatly, "He can't be, if he's a local outlaw. Whatever this is all about, it can hardly involve the theft of cows. It makes more sense if Johnny Two Hats recruited local help. The breed was the one they planted with Maxwell Windsor's party in the first place. I'd say it's more likely your local boy was just hired to hold pony reins and such by the real pro the master-mind hired. I gunned another, over to Sheridan the other day. So he might be getting a mite short-handed. If we can take Scribe Henderson alive, he might be able to tell us who Johnny Two Hats was working for. Then again, he might not. I don't want you and yours taking needless chances with a man we know to be a cornered-rat fighter. The law in Warren just found out the hard way that taking him alive could be a bother."

Big Joe patted the big S&W on his hip and growled, "I wasn't figuring on a protracted conversation with the cuss if he comes back this way. He gets one chance to grab for the sky. Then me and mine mean to lay him low if he hesitates at all."

Longarm nodded, sipped more suds, and said, "You have the advantage of knowing what he looks like. I don't. Would you happen to have any pictures of the cuss on hand?"

Big Joe shook his head morosely and replied, "It's hard to get a gent like Scribe Henderson to hold that still. He's never been arrested. They just found out why, in Warren. Up until now he was only wanted for stealing stock and beating up a whore in Basin. I think the B.I.A. wants him for molesting Indian gals. Now that he's wanted for killing that deputy in Warren, he's likely to become more famous."

"More *scarce,* too, if he's got a lick of sense," Longarm said. "You say he got in trouble with the law in Basin, Wyoming Territory? I thought he was a Montana rider, Big Joe."

The older lawman grimaced. "Riders follow the lay of the land more than they do imaginary lines across a map they ain't reading. The Bighorn Basin, north and south of the line, is Scribe Henderson's chosen field of crookery. He's said to hide out betwixt jobs up in the Montana hills above the Yellowstone. He works down this way with the gangs preying on the trail herds through this basin. Ain't no trailing going on right now, so no doubt that was why he hired out with the gang you're after."

Longarm said, "I'm hoping it's more like a fistful of sneaks than a gang. If Scribe Henderson has a hideout way to the north, that's likely where he's headed, unless the late Johnny Two Hats told him more than he should have. Just in case I'm wrong, what does the rascal look like?"

"Innocent," Big Joe said. "It's hard to steal beef regular when you look like someone on the cover of a Ned Buntline magazine. He's tall, about your height, only skinnier. Smooth-shaven, at least once a week, and wears his hair as short as most hands. He

83

dresses honest cowboy and wears one gun, high and cross-draw, like you, come to study on it. I can't say what brand of gun it might be, save that it's double-action and throws .45. Don't most honest hands pack a .44, come to study on it?"

Longarm nodded. "I do, for the same reason. Winchester don't make a carbine chambered .45 and it's a bother packing two kinds of ammunition. The army, Texas Rangers, and some hired killers favor .45s because when you can't put a ball in a man where it really matters, the extra shock may slow him down enough to hold still for a second round."

"How come you figure a .44-40 is enough to do the job? Never mind, stupid question. I'd hate to get hit with a *.22* if it was *you* aiming at me."

Longarm didn't answer. He wasn't given to bragging about his marksmanship. Junior Briggs joined his father and Longarm to say, "Some of the boys was just studying on that nigger who worked for that artist along with the breed I had to gun today. Has it occurred to you that *both* the missing man's servants must have turned on him?"

Longarm shook his head. "It don't work as simple mutiny, Junior. Aside from the fact that the valet—I think his name was James—has been with Mr. Windsor some time, it's sort of unusual for servants to murder and rob their employer and then hang around pegging shots at the law near the scene of the crime."

Junior opined, "Some niggers are sort of dumb, you know."

Longarm said, "Dumb or smart, a colored gent is *noticeable* in these parts. If old James was in on some sort of plot, where might he be right now, and how come nobody's mentioned seeing him? Like his

84

boss and that red river cart, he seems to have vanished somewhere between here and wherever."

Junior asked, "What if him and the breed turned on the white artist gent, killed him, robbed him, hid both him and his fool cart good, and simply lit out?"

"That was one of the first notions I came up with," Longarm said. "For who knows how a servant might or might not feel about his boss, no matter how long he's worked for him? But look at her this way, Junior. Windsor wasn't traveling with a whole lot of money. Certainly not as much as his valet could have robbed him of at home, back East, years ago. The paintings in that cart might be worth something to a slick and clever crook but, again, we're stuck with the simple fact that James could have stolen a whole studio full before they ever came out here. And, assuming he was smart enough to get away with selling the works of a famous living artist, how come he'd be dumb enough to do it so complicated and then *hang around?* It's this hanging around that's got me so puzzled. For, while I can think of all kinds of devious doings, not a one makes any sense at all to me. If Windsor is still alive and well, how come nobody's heard from him all this time? If he *ain't* alive and well, how come it's so important to someone that I don't find him, one damned way or the other?"

Big Joe asked, "What if he's alive but not well? What if he's been kidnapped, and the ones holding him are afraid you'll rescue him?"

Longarm inhaled more suds as he studied on that. Then he said, "Crooks generally have a *reason* for holding anyone prisoner. If ransom was their motive, someone should have gotten a ransom demand by now."

"What if the family was told not to tell the law or they'd kill the old gent?" Junior suggested.

Longarm started to object. Then he said, "Out of the mouths of babes, no offense. It's true Windsor's kith and kin contacted us to look for him before *we* knew he was missing. But they *could* have received such a note, more recent, and not seen fit to tell us about it. I can see I got to send me some more wires, now. It's been nice talking to you, gents."

As he left for the Western Union across the way, Junior Briggs tagged along. Outside, he said, "There's something else I'd like to talk over with you, in private, Longarm."

"About that gent you shot earlier?"

"Yeah. How did you know?"

"The first man I ever shot was a boy younger than you. It was fair enough. I was just as young, and he was pointing a rifle at me at a place called Shiloh. It was about this time after sundown that I got to feeling funny about it. If you ever have to gun another person, it won't confuse you as much, Junior. Let's hope you'll never be the sort of man who *enjoys* such thrills. But once you've felt that funny feeling, it won't *surprise* you so much, see?"

The younger lawman said, "It ain't that I feels bad or guilty. I done what I had to, and he was a no-good killer. It's just that, now that I've really killed a man, I feel so unusually, well, *usual!*"

Longarm nodded and told him gently, "I said I've been there. One part of you keeps saying, My God, I've killed a man, and that must make me a killer! But, try as you might, you don't feel no different. It seems as if you ought to sprout horns or at least more hair on your chest, now that you've become a gent who can say he's killed another. But you're still the same old boy you always was. No better. No worse, as far as you can tell. I reckon to men looking *forward* to the experience it must feel a letdown. Maybe that's why some men just keep killing, as if they expect it to be wonderful. You'd think, after a while, they'd learn to stop. Killing ain't a way to enjoy life. It's a chore like any other, when there just ain't no way of getting out of it."

Junior Briggs didn't answer for a few paces. Then he said, "I reckon you *must* have been at Shiloh. I was worried that I might have something wrong with me. You descripted my feelings exactsome, though. It's sure nice to learn I ain't no freak."

Longarm chuckled. "You'd be a freak if you felt like flapping your wings and crowing, or mayhaps like bending over for a whipping, Junior. You're going to be all right. It's the gents as get *excited,* either way, you got to worry about."

They parted friendly at the Western Union doorway and Longarm went in to ask for some telegram blanks.

The middle-aged clerk on night duty handed some across the counter, saying, "I got a recent message for you from your home office, Deputy Long."

He handed that over as well. Longarm tore it open and read it twice, trying to make sense out of it. The old-timer said, "I'm sorry about the words they blanked out. We ain't allowed to send cuss words along the wire, and your boss sure seems to have a pungent vocabulary."

Longarm smiled thinly and replied, "That ain't what I find so confusing. Marshal Vail must have been confused enough to cuss that much as well. It seems that thieves busted into the Denver Museum of Modern Art to steal just one fool picture. Poor old Billy Vail seems to hope I can figure out why."

"Can you, Deputy Long?"

"Not hardly. That artist I'm searching for is popular as hell, but his pictures don't sell for the prices Renoir and Monet get. Yet the thieves passed up a fortune in modern art to swipe the one bitty Maxwell Windsor they had hanging on their wall. Ain't that a bitch?"

Chapter 8

Longarm had resigned himself to at least a few tedious days and enjoyable nights in Hillsboro. But the next morning they got a wire from the county coronor, saying someone had to be loco if they thought he had time to waste on varmint shooting by paid-up county peace officers. So Longarm was free to ride on.

Before he did, he told Big Joe Briggs about the burglary in Denver and suggested the Maxwell Windsor painting the widow Grant had been given by the artist might hang safer in the town lockup for now. Big Joe said he liked the notion of a stakeout better. Longarm shook his head and told him, "The gal could get hurt. If you want to set someone up as bait, what say you borrow the landscape from her for now and make sure everyone in town hears it's hanging on *your* wall?"

Big Joe said that was jake with him if the widow gal would go along with it. Longarm said he'd talk to her about it. Then he and the Western Union clerk had to figure out a way to wire the Crow Indian Police. There was no telegraph line between Hillsboro and the agency, but since electricity could whip all over creation, fast as light, the clerk figured the fewest number of relay points and Longarm was able to send a warning to Laughing Raven. As he thanked the helpful clerk, he explained, "I sort of hope the skunks *try* to purloin some paintings up that way. Us pale lawmen ain't allowed to scalp burglars."

He went back to the hotel to settle up with old Sandra. She was a good sport about it, even if she did get sort of weepy before he could get upstairs for his gear. He told her about the painting she had and the possible danger it might put her in. She said she'd work things out about the painting with Big Joe, later, as Longarm suggested. Then she followed him up the stairs and pestered him about the art theft in Denver. He'd already told her as much as he knew. She seemed to think it was important that the stolen picture had been a portrait of the missing artist's daughter.

"Now, you can't say for sure what *any* of 'em really look like, right?" she asked.

By this time they were in his hired room, so he was able to reply, "Wrong. Along with all the tedious paperwork, I have the tin and paper photographs the daughter sent us when she first reported her daddy missing."

He opened one saddlebag and rummaged the manila envelope out, adding, "There's no photograph of the late Johnny Two Hats, of course. But we ain't looking for him no more, so that don't matter. I got a fair-sized print of Windsor, himself, and family tintypes showing him, his daughter, and even that colored servant. Here, I'll show 'em to you, and— Damn it, Sandra, you can't have your wicked way with me now."

But she was awfully pretty, and they both knew it was unlikely they'd get to do it ever again. So as she proceeded to peel entire he put the envelope back in the saddlebag. He figured, afterwards, that as long as the day was half shot, he might as well just lie there smoking a spell, with her head on his bare shoulder. But when she started toying with his privates again he warned her sternly, "You could be interfering with justice, girl. For I really got to go look for poor old Windsor some more."

She said, "Pooh! If he was within two days' ride of here our own riders would have found him by this time. You want to know what I think? I think he was never missing out here at all. I think he finished his paintings of the West and just caught the train back East in Lovell, Gray Bull, or Basin."

Longarm started to tell her she was loco, but he was a fair-minded pillow talker, so he said, "Well, that would explain why nobody down that way reported him in their vicinity if, say, he and his valet just hopped a train some time ago, before they was reported missing."

She toyed with the hair on his belly as she pointed out, "If he's not missing at all, you could surely find more interesting things to do than search for him out in that hot sun, couldn't you, darling?"

He laughed. "I wasn't looking forward to riding on. But folk are hardly ever reported missing when they ain't. If them gents caught a train back East, weeks ago, they'd have been home long before Windsor's kin asked us to look for 'em."

She insisted, "It's more likely his daughter just fibbed to you all to cover up some bodies buried in a New York root cellar. She did it so's she could inherit all her rich father's money. Is this thing getting harder or softer? I can't tell."

He growled, "Let go of my poor abused flesh and tell me why you'd want to talk so dirty about another gal who's never even seen it. I know you're just funning, honey. But even in fun, it ain't Christian to make such serious charges in the company of a peace officer."

She said, "Call it intuition or call it jealousy, but the only reason I can think of for that portrait being stolen is that they don't want you or other lawmen to *see* it."

He laughed incredulously. "I already have. It's been there a spell and it's got its very own catalogue number. It was painted years ago and fuzzy besides. There's no mystery as to what everyone from the Windsor household might look like. And, even if your dreadful suspicion about the poor little gal was right, she'd have to be dumb as hell to kill her own father and then report him missing to draw the law's attention to the deed."

But Sandra had gotten on top, by then. So as he rose to the occasion inside her he put her wild suspicions aside for the time being. But later, before he rode out of town, he wired Billy Vail that it might be a good notion to check with the New York police and make sure for certain that Maxwell Windsor was missing out *this* way instead of back *that* way.

He covered another bet by fording the Bighorn to ride south, upstream, along the bank fewer riders followed. He knew the well-worn trail west of the river had been searched, more than once, by at least a few old boys who had to be tolerable at reading sign.

But all he noticed on the far side of the river, as he rode the buckskin and led the black, was that even a greenhorn would have to be dumb as hell to push a red river cart through so much mud and tanglewood.

Longarm found a winding game trail and followed it. It was hard to tell whether travel was more difficult on this side because it had always been or whether the clearing of streamside growth for firewood on the west bank had dried and firmed things up. Either way, it was rougher going. There were stretches where spurs of the Bighorn Range to the east came down to the water's edge and the game trail circled up into tall timber to avoid stream-washed slick-rock. As he rode he naturally kept an eye peeled for old campfires or even patches where someone might have busted through the firm carpets of pine needle or orchard grass. Just as naturally, he didn't spot any. No grave six weeks old would have been dug with enough sign to matter, but the only way one could bury a red river cart involved a mighty big hole in the ground.

It was around four in the afternoon when he came to a wall of house-sized boulders blocking further progress south. He paused to swap saddles and eat a can of tomatoes he'd bought in Hillsboro while the ponies grazed and rested a mite.

Then he mounted the black mare and told her, "I know it would make more sense to cross back over to the sensible side. But we're detouring up and around this rock pile, anyways. For if I was a treacherous guide I might or might not turn on my employer way upslope in tall timber. I sure can't come up with a better place, hereabouts."

Leading the buckskin, he rode up and up until they were in broody dark lodgepole pine patched with glades of prettier but buggier aspen. They found a break in the rocky cross-grain outcrop and, better yet, a trail that, while hardly a wagon trace, looked wide enough for a red river cart. It was running more or less back down toward the river, so Longarm followed it. He had only followed it three-quarters of a mile when someone shot his hat off and the woods all around echoed to rebel yells and such friendly suggestions as "Get him! Kill him! Don't let the son of a bitch get away!"

By this time, of course, Longarm was afoot and had dragged both his ponies after him into an aspen thicket. He couldn't get his ponies to flatten out without shooting them, which would have been sort of pointless, so he tethered them deep in the dense growth and eased back the way he had led them, levering a round into the chamber of his Winchester as he heard someone shouting, "Git downwind and see if you can set them aspen afire, Jeb."

Longarm grinned wolfishly as he tested the faint breeze with a wet finger and proceeded to move into it, Indian style. Aspen was hard to burn, even in a stove. So he soon sniffed the considerable effort someone was putting into setting the greenwoods afire with damp newspaper and kitchen matches. Longarm worked his way through the densely growing aspen trunks until he could see the two gents hunkered in the smoke of their own making before he took cover behind a fair-sized double tree, forked at ground level, to call out low and casually, considering, "You'd need coal oil to do that right, boys. But you'd best stomp that smoulder out, as you grab some sky, in any case."

The two men froze, staring wildly about for the source of his voice. "I'm over here, with the drop on you, and I don't mean to mention the sky again, you arsonistical sons of bitches," he went on.

They both got to their feet, hands high, as the younger of them pleaded, "Don't gun us, Scribe. We was just trying to do our duty. It was never meant to spite you personal."

Longarm grimaced. "I'd sure hate to be in dry timber with you boys really *mad* at me. How come you just addressed me by the name of Scribe?"

"Ain't you Scribe Henderson, the gent we was wired to head off?"

"Oh, for Gawd's sake, what made you think I might be him?"

"We spotted you from across the river a spell

94

back, Mr. Henderson. If you'll promise not to do us like you done that deputy in Warren I'll tell you why you're so easy to recognize at a distance, and what you can do about it."

Longarm looked disgusted and replied, "Henderson was leading an extra pony packing a *riding* saddle, you assholes. You can lower your hands, now, but keep 'em polite. I'm law, too. I ride for Uncle Sam as U.S. Deputy Custis Long. Now I want you to call that out to the rest of the posse before someone gets hurt around here."

The two men he had the drop on exchanged glances. Then the older one called out, "Hey, Jake? There's a gent here who's got the drop on us, and he says he ain't Scribe Henderson at all!"

Longarm swore softly and added, "If I was an owlhoot, you'd be dead already. Call it *right*, you silly bastard!"

The younger one shouted, "He says he's a federal deputy, and I think he means it, boys. We'd best all hold our fire for now!"

Nothing happened. As he heard a twig snap somewhere off to his left, Longarm said, "All right. Listen tight and keep an eye on the muzzle of this Winchester. I'm reaching for my badge. I aim to toss it your way. Then I want you to sound a whole lot more convincing. For, if they creep in any closer, I may commence to suspicion *your* story as well."

He opened his wallet and tossed it out between them. It landed open with the badge up, bless it. The one closest to him took a cautious step his way, stared down, and yelled out, "Hey, Jake? It's all right! He's really who he says he is, and old Stubby can't sneak for shit in aspen!"

Longarm could tell from the less cautious crashes all about that it was safe to step out in the open and pick up his wallet as the tension eased.

They were soon joined by close to two dozen men moving in from every direction through the trees. Jake turned out to be a middle-aged county deputy who didn't look too intelligent even when he was trying to look friendly. He seemed to think it was a good joke on him that they'd mistaken Longarm at a distance for a fugitive killer. They were all from Kane Township, they said. Longarm half closed his eyes to read his mental map of the big basin and said, "Right. That would be the jerkwater stop and general store where the tracks part company with the river to get to Lovell. I didn't know there was a Western Union there, no offense."

Jake said, "There ain't. The railroad telegrapher relayed the all-points to us a few hours ago. We was just saddling up when a kid atop the water tower seen you passing on the far bank and we been laying for you some time. What took you so long?"

"I ate lunch. In other words, I'm farther south than Lovell or Kane, and what's the next town south?"

"On this side of the river? Nothing for a good forty miles or more. The settlement of Manderson is on this side, down past the county seat. You'll never make her a third of the way this side of nightfall. Why don't you come on back to Kane with us and we'll all have us a drink to our good fortune. That murderous Scribe Henderson don't seem to be headed this way, after all."

Longarm said, "I won't get far, soon, if I keep backtracking for the comforts of civilization, no offense. So I'd best push on. I ain't after Henderson, direct. I suppose you boys has heard of that missing artist and his party?"

"Sure we has," Jake said. "We may be sort of out in the country, but we ain't *total* rubes. We got the all-points on him some time ago. He never come through Kane. Is that why you've been looking on this side of the water?"

Longarm nodded. "Yeah, and you're right about how late it's getting."

He started to move back to his ponies. Then he turned with a thoughtful frown and said, "Let's see if I got this straight in my head. We're holding this discussion in Bighorn County, Wyoming Territory, right?"

Jake nodded. "I sure hope so. Why?"

Longarm said, "Unless I read the map wrong, last time I looked, both Warren and Hillsboro lie just north of the Montana line. So Henderson smoked up them other lawmen and Junior Briggs smoked up his pal, Johnny Two Hats, outside the jurisdiction of Bighorn County."

Jake shrugged and said, "I could have told you that. What difference does that make?"

Longarm frowned and mused half to himself, "I know neither territory is incorporated as a self-regulating state, yet, and I've seen the law regulated sort of casual where folk *do* get to elect their own state government. But ain't both Hillsboro and Warren in Carbon County, Montana, and don't Carbon County have any sheriff at all?"

"Sure they do. Who do you reckon wired us to be on the lookout for Scribe Henderson? Them was Carbon County deputies he shot it out with up to Warren. So what?"

"So Big Joe Briggs said he'd reported the killing of Johnny Two Hats to Bighorn County, here on the Wyoming side of the line. I can see, now, why Basin Township wired back they wasn't interested. The shooting should have been reported to another coroner entire."

Jake shrugged. "Oh, Big Joe Briggs is all right. He has kin here in Bighorn County," he told Longarm.

Another posse rider opined, "I can answer such a

pesky nit pick. Hillsboro may be in Montana Territory, officious, but it's still in the Bighorn Basin, sliverized betwixt the Crow Reserve and our county line. You can't wire direct to Red Lodge on the Clark Fork from Hillsboro. Red Lodge may be the officious county seat of Hillsboro, but nobody up that way pays much attention to that. Us Bighorn Basin boys all sort of stick together, and, hell, we're discussing outlaws who draws even *less* fine distinctions."

Longarm agreed he could be splitting hairs. They shook and parted friendly. But by the time Longarm was riding south alone again, he was almost of a mind to turn around and ride back for some answers.

He decided it was too far, considering such answers as he was likely to get, and how hard it would be to get away from old Sandra again, after dark.

But it was still one hell of a way to run things, even in a barely settled corner of the so-called Wild West. It hardly seemed likely Big Joe and Junior Briggs had been trying to put anything sneaky over on him. Others in Hillsboro had seen the Windsor party pass through town safely. But Junior had proven himself an inexperienced young lawman who'd never had to draw his gun before, and if his fool father didn't know a thing about legal jurisdiction *he* didn't add up as much of a bloodhound, either.

The posse he'd just run into had been a glorified lynch mob of cowhands led by yet another lawman who wasn't qualified to be a night watchman anywhere crime was at all serious. So, as he reined in on a grassy rise to rest his mount a spell, he told her, "It's small wonder that artistic gent seems to have vanished so mysterious in these parts. For, despite all the reassurances, and in all modesty, I seem to be the very first real lawman with a lick of professional training who's even *looked* for him!"

Chapter 9

As the sun went down, the moon rose bright enough
for riding but hardly bright enough for reading sign,
and Longarm had already had his hat shot off one
time on that tricky trail. So he rode upslope into a
tongue of pines, found a clearing well padded with
their dry needles, and prepared to bed down for the
night.

After he had made his ponies secure as well as
comfortable, he cleared pine duff down to bare dirt
and built a small Indian cook fire. He had chosen the
cover with that in mind. He could live on uncooked
provisions if he had to. He didn't need coffee to put
himself to sleep. But nothing beat black coffee on
top of a warm breakfast to get a man going in the
cold gray dawn, and he'd been making poor time up
to now.

He rolled out his bedding and leaned against his
grounded saddle to have a smoke as he waited for the
windfall pine knots he had gathered to simmer down
to decent cooking coals. Then he broke out a cast-
iron spider, some fatback and flour, and made flap-
jacks for supper. Having neither butter nor syrup to

put on them, he only made enough to settle his innards. He washed them down with just enough coffee for now and, as the fire died, he got up to heed the call of nature among the trees down the slope. As he moved back up the slope, he heard one of his ponies nicker and paused to ponder some about that.

Indian ponies, like Indian dogs, were trained to remain sedate after dark in camp unless they had a serious reason for sounding off. Of course, while a Crow was likely to have a yappy pup for supper, a pony broke in peacetime, and issued to a white man in any case, could just be making conversation with an owl bird or pack rat. But Longarm drew his Colt as he moved in soundlessly.

So the next sound anyone heard was the roar of yet another sixgun, close, five times and then a click as the hammer fell on an empty chamber. The dark figure who had made such a racket was standing over Longarm's bedroll, smoking gun in hand, when the bemused lawman told him, politely but in dead earnest, "Drop it and freeze."

The stranger who had just blown five holes through Longarm's bedding heaved a sad little sigh, muttered, "Aw, shit!" and let go his sixgun to see how many pine branches he could grab without actually jumping for them. Longarm stayed where he was as he said conversationally, "I can see you don't enjoy getting shot. I must say that's sort of disappointing. Now I want you to tell me true if we're alone out here. For, if I catch you fibbing, you'll be lucky as hell to just wind up dead."

The other man said, "It's just you and me, Longarm."

His captor replied grimly, "I figured them rounds you just put in my bedroll had to be meant for someone you knew and admired. Don't turn around. Put your right hand down behind you, first, so's I can cuff it. Then put your left down . . . Aw, hell, you must have been arrested before, right?"

As he cuffed his prisoner, the rascal allowed that, as a matter of fact, he was finding this a new and hardly enjoyable experience. Longarm held the chain links between the cuffed fists with his own free hand to frog march his prisoner face first into a tree trunk before he spun him around in the moonlight, nodded, and decided, "You'd be Scribe Henderson. For if anyone else as likely to gun me in my sleep described as ugly as you I'd have heard about him by now. You must know you face a hanging for that deputy in Warren. There's no way I can get you off for that. On the other hand, as a federal prisoner, they can't have you until after I'm done with you. So just how useful to me do you feel like behaving?"

Henderson sighed and answered. "Well, I'd do just about anything to keep from swinging *country* style."

"I'd sure like to hear who sent you after me and what in thunder this is all about," Longarm told him.

Scribe Henderson grimaced and said, "Hell, that ain't no big mystery. You gunned my pal, Johnny, up to Hillsboro. I didn't come way down here to get revenge, exactly. But when I seen I had the chance, all right, I *took* it. Satisfied?"

"Not hardly. You was last seen in Warren, way the hell northwest of here. So, for openers, how come our trails crossed down this way? How did you know who I was when they did, or do you always gun total strangers in bed on the outside chance it could be someone you wasn't fond of?"

Scribe Henderson looked sort of pleased with himself as he said, "I was listening when you talked to Jake Yager back there. You see, I was sort of tagging along with the posse that was after me. I was in the general store at Kane when they commenced to gather to go after me. I figured the best place to be at such a dismal time would be riding *with* 'em, so——"

"I didn't *think* old Jake looked too smart," Longarm cut in. "It's an old trick. But it often works when a mess of riders who don't know one another all that well posse up. I'll allow you're slicker than the local law. It stands to reason you'd have to be. Now you're going to tell me who you and the late Johnny Two Hats was working for, ain't you?"

Henderson replied, "Johnny asked me, personal, to throw in with him. We'd stole cows afore, a few years back, afore he had to go back East for his . . . ah . . . health. We run into each other in the saloon in Basin and——*Jeee-zusss!*"

Longarm stood calmly holding the smoking muzzle of his gun on the frightened owlhoot as the sound of his casual shot echoed away amid the trees. Longarm had aimed just above his prisoner's head on purpose, but as bark and pine gum rained from the still quivering brim of Henderson's hat, Longarm muttered, "I never should have filed my front sight down for a fast draw, I reckon."

The owlhoot cowered against the pine trunk, pleading, "I ain't holding out on you, damn it!"

Longarm smiled thinly. "Sure you are. I asked you who you was working for and you told me a big fib."

"Don't shoot, damn it! Johnny did allow he was working for a gent who wanted you dead. I can tell you it wasn't the dude he was with, or the nigger they had along with 'em. Johnny had hired on as a guide with orders to just lead them around until further orders. He said the nigger got sick, somewhere betwixt Kane and Basin, and had to be left ahint at some cow spread. He said that when they got to Basin the old gent who owned the wagon was feeling poorly, too, or mayhaps just discouraged. Anyway, when the old gent paid Johnny off and said he'd seed enough of the country out here, Johnny wired for further instructions and they told him you was crowding the old gent too close and that they wanted him to do something about it. He was still wondering how he ought to go about that when he met up with me again and . . . knowing I had some experience along them lines, offered to cut me in on the bounty on you."

Longarm cocked an eyebrow and asked, "Do tell? How much am I worth, dead, these days?"

"Johnny said they'd give us a thousand to split, after. When we got up to the Indian Agency to lay for you, you was just leaving. So we followed, looking for a crack at you. I told him it was dumb to go into town after you like that. But when you rid in and seemed to take so long riding out, old Johnny just couldn't wait. The rest you know. When I heard Johnny was dead I figured it was time to hop a train out of the basin. You know what happened when I rid into a stakeout in Warren, too. So I was making my way back for Basin Township, hoping to meet up with Johnny's boss, when I wound up riding with that posse, seen yet another chance to collect that bounty, and—"

The gun in Longarm's hand went off again. This time Scribe Henderson lost an earlobe and, to hear the way he carried on, one might have thought he'd been hit *serious*.

He fell to his knees at Longarm's feet, hands cuffed behind him, to sob, "I swear on my mother's head that I ain't been lying to you, Longarm!"

Longarm growled, "You must not think much of your poor old mother, then. Your tale has more holes in it than a miner's sock. How the hell did you ever figure on putting in for the money on *my* head if you don't know who the master-mind might be?"

Henderson whined, "I never, for certain. But Johnny said he'd pointed me out, discreet, to the folk he was working for and told 'em I was their sort of boy. I figured, did I just go on back and hang about the same saloon until word come in about . . . well, about the way things was *supposed* to work out here this evening, they'd contact *me*, see?"

Longarm had to pay for his own bullets. So this time he just pistol-whipped the cow thief flat, growling, "That's only one hole in the sock you're trying to darn. The timing is all wrong. Maxwell Windsor has been missing over a month, and you're trying to tell me all this business with that breed just started a few days ago? Where's this cow spread where the sick colored man is supposed to be staying? Where in Basin has old Maxwell Windsor been holed up all this time, if the breed last saw him alive and well?"

Henderson sat up, spitting blood and pine needles, to insist, "You're asking the wrong man, damn it! I never seen *any* of the gents you're looking for. Maybe Johnny lied to me. It ain't as if he had his hand on no Bible, and he wasn't exactly famous for his truthsome nature."

"Try her this way," Longarm suggested, "Say the breed *murdered* his boss and the faithful servant, almost anywhere, now that I've seen how good the others looking for him really are. Say the kith and kin of the missing artist started the search for him too early and too close to where the deed was done. Say the master-mind was less interested in having Windsor's body found than the folk who was really worried about him. Johnny Two Hats wasn't the only one as tried to stop me from getting this far. We both know he was better known as a thief than a killer, even though he did attempt to branch out more than he should have. How do you like him sitting on all the valuable paintings from that red river cart, until he got word that killing me was more important?"

The prisoner shrugged and said, "I ain't never going to argue with you no more, you infernal fiend. I never seen no infernal art works. I just hired on to do a job I now see as piss-poor pay, even if we'd gotten you. Is it true that federal hangmen ain't allowed to do it mean and slow, like some county part-timers?"

"I'll decide who gets to hang you after I know you better," Longarm said. Then he hauled Henderson to his feet and spun him around again, adding, "Now I aim to cuff you to this tree so's I can get some sleep."

As he did so, Henderson complained, "Hey, how am *I* supposed to get any rest, halfways crucified in the cold night air like this?"

Longarm said, "Oh, you can hunker some, if you set your mind to it. Think of all the rest you'll get once I hand you over."

A gray jay woke Longarm at dawn. He rolled out, washed up, and rebuilt his fire as the camp-robbing jays plotted against him on the branches all about. Scribe Henderson was complaining that he hadn't slept a wink as Longarm led him to the fire and cuffed his hands in front of him so he wouldn't have to be fed like a baby. As he did so, Longarm warned the wild-eyed, weak-chinned Henderson, "Don't try to take advantage of my kindness if you value your kneecaps. I know that you know any chance a man might take beats no chance at all, and that a clean shot can't hurt no worse than hanging. That's why I tell you boys I don't feel obligated to kill an escaping prisoner *total*."

Henderson promised to keep Longarm's advice in mind. The lawman broke out some of the grub he'd purchased in Hillsboro. The bacon was all right. It smelled good sizzling in the spider and they only lost one slice to a show-off gray jay who wound up with smouldering wing tips and tail features for a prize that wasn't worth it, to hear him cussing from an overhead branch as he tried to figure out what he'd grabbed from the hot grease.

They had assured Longarm at the general store that the half-dozen eggs he'd taken a chance on were local-laid, water-glass-dipped, and had to be good for at least a few more days. The first one he broke open smelled horrible, so he scrambled it with a less disgusting one and politely fed his prisoner first. When the would-be murderer protested, Longarm said not to eat it if he wasn't hungry and added, "Had it been up to you, right about now I'd be enjoying a mouthful of blow-flies for breakfast. You'll be lucky to get grits and gravy where *you're* going."

Henderson protested that he liked cream and sugar in his coffee as well, so Longarm got to drink most of the Arbuckle he brewed that morning. Then he cuffed his prisoner's hands behind him again and told him to play church-mouse until the stock was saddled and ready to go.

He put Henderson's saddle on the somewhat spooky black mare and the packsaddle on Henderson's bay. When the killer commented on this, Longarm explained, "You'll play hell guiding my mare, here, with your knees alone. I know because I've tried. I mean to ride the buckskin, because he's more steady if I have to fire from the saddle. Your own critter can act any way he wants to as long as he don't fight the lead rope. You sure have a cruel bit in that Mex bridle, and now I'd best get you aboard first, you mean-hearted son of a bitch."

Henderson protested that he was afraid he would fall off if he had to ride with his hands behind him.

Longarm boosted him up anyway, saying, "Try to land on your head so you can't get hurt."

Then he made double sure the fire was out, mounted the buckskin, and they were on their way with Longarm in the lead, Henderson in the middle, and the pack pony trailing.

They forded back across the Bighorn for several good reasons. Longarm's main one was that while the late Johnny Two Hats may or may not have told the truth about the colored valet being left at some cattle spread, he had mentioned cattle spreads, and there just weren't any along the east bank of the river. This was no doubt because there was still plenty of room to pick and choose from in the Bighorn Basin and there was more cover for beasts of prey, on four legs or less, between the river and the nearby foothills. The Front Ranges to the west were much farther off, leaving the range more open, west of the river. The rail line that now followed the west bank made it a more sensible side to raise beef for profit, too.

But while Longarm spotted stock all around—mostly calico Texas cows that spooked easy and didn't graze too close to the railroad tracks Longarm was more or less following—he failed to spy any spreads that close to the tracks and river. The banks were now deep as well as steep in places. Henderson said that some years the spring floods washed over the rails atop the even higher roadbed. Longarm believed him and found that a sensible enough reason for building well back from the river. Now and again he spotted chimney smoke above a rise to the west. But since Henderson said he had no idea which if any spread that colored man might be staying at, Longarm let that notion go for now. The valet had had plenty of time to either die or get better. Either event should have caused some local gossip Longarm could pick up later.

It was a pleasant day for riding. The service road alongside the tracks was sun-baked firm and not too dusty, so by noon they made it into the hamlet of Gray Bull, or Greybull, as the sign above the post office spelled it. Either way, the place was named for the mountain stream that required a railroad trestle there as it poured into the Bighorn at right angles. The stream, in turn, was named for a recent and mighty mean Indian who'd done something awful in the Shining Times. Nobody in the tiny town named for him offered any history lessons. The more recent events up the tracks in Warren held their undivided interest. They told Longarm the railroad trestle offered a grand opportunity to hold a high noon public hanging. But he said he had to decline, as tempting as their notion was. Some ladies served him and his prisoner coffee and cake.

Nobody in Gray Bull had heard anything about a colored man, dead or alive, staying at any of the surrounding spreads. Like the local livestock, most of the folk in the basin seemed to have followed the Goodnight–Loving Trail up from Texas as the northern ranges were cleared of buffalo and Mister Lo. So Longarm knew they weren't being ugly on purpose when they assured him they'd keep an eye out for "that poor nigger." Few of them had ever known free folk of color well enough to know how much they objected to such terms.

Getting across the Gray Bull, unless you were a railroad train, was easier said than done. Longarm had to ride alongside his prisoner and steady him as they rode down the steep bank, across the churning stirrup-deep stream, and up the just-as-steep far side. Then they were on their way to the county seat again with time to spare. Longarm figured they'd make it

108

well before three that afternoon at the rate they were going. The service road had widened to an obviously well-traveled go-to-town by now. The sun was getting hotter, but there was a cool mountain breeze from the west, just brisk enough to carry the perfumes of rabbit-bush, greasewood, and sage without stirring up dust or spooking the ponies.

Longarm figured they were about an hour north of Basin Township when, as they approached yet another wooded draw winding cross-grained into the Bighorn, his prisoner announced that he needed to heed the call of nature.

Longarm asked, "Can't you hold it? We're almost there, and they're sure to have a more civilized crapper in the jailhouse."

But Henderson insisted. Longarm grumbled. But, come to study on it, the coffee he had had in Gray Bull might have been in him long enough. So, when the roadway dipped down into the draw, he led the way up the dry streambed until they were at a discreet distance from the public thoroughfare. He reined in, dismounted, and helped Henderson down. He said, "I'll unbuckle and unbutton you, but I'll be damned if I'll hold it for you."

He dropped Henderson's pants for him, noting the owlhoot wore no underdrawers, and strode off to water his own cottonwood as the owlhoot hunkered down. But just as he was fixing to relieve himself, Longarm heard something buzzing in the grass and dry leaves at his feet and instinctively flinched the other way, just in time. He never found out whether that had been a rattler or just a prairie locust pretending to be one. The yard-long arrow that had thudded into the tree trunk he'd been about to pee against seemed a lot more important to Longarm as he dove headfirst into the waist-high clump of rabbit-bush, rolled even farther on the far side, and got behind a fallen log with his sidearm in hand, even if he didn't know where his *hat* might be just now.

A million years went by as he strained his ears to hear a leaf fall here and a bird chirp there. He'd have suspected himself of spooking at shadows if he couldn't see, from where he crouched, the feathered end of the arrow some son of a bitch had aimed so seriously at his back. He knew the first rule in Indian fighting was to let them guess where you might be. But he had his prisoner to consider, and the relatives of the late Johnny Two Hats didn't figure to be Hungarians or Greeks!

Cautiously, making no more noise than he could manage to avoid in summer-dry grass and brush, Longarm edged around to the west, since that was the way he would have come from had he been left over from Gray Bull's band. Indians packing bows and arrows hardly ever rode railroad trains. He worked his way to a view down the clearer center of the draw. Then he didn't know whether to laugh or cuss. For Scribe Henderson sure looked comical with his bare ass sticking up like that, although the arrow in the back of his shirt wasn't all that funny.

Longarm made sure his back was covered by thick tanglewood before he called out, "Heya! If you are men, show yourselves so we can have a good fight!"

It didn't work. He tried, "I know your nation. You have to be Pawnee. Everyone know Pawnee are afraid to die. That's why they let their mothers fight for them."

That was neither fair nor true. But since he didn't know who in thunder the arrow-pushing sons of bitches might be, he'd picked a distant nation both the Crow and their local enemies had always hated. Like some white men, Pawnee seemed to feel it best to shoot any other breed of humankind on sight. They had some religious notions most other Indians

110

found disgusting as well. But, though Longarm repeated his taut and threw in some remarks about what his unseen enemy's mother might be doing when she wasn't fighting for her cowardly sons, he failed to even draw another arrow.

Another million years went by. By this time Longarm had worked back to the ponies, picking up his hat along the way. All three ponies were calmly browsing cottonwood leaves and the birds in the branches above had calmed down as well. An Indian who didn't steal a pony when he had its owner dead or pinned down was either not an Indian or not around any more. So Longarm quietly took his long-delayed leak, led the ponies back to the roadway, and got out of there.

Chapter 10

After he got to the county seat, Longarm left all three ponies at the livery near the courthouse and paid a courtesy call on the local sheriff. He wound up talking to a senior deputy named Haydock, an older lawman who explained the sheriff was away on personal business involving beef. When Longarm brought him up to date on his recent adventures, Haydock said he was pleased to hear Scribe Henderson was dead, but mighty surprised to hear the way he had died. Haydock said, "We ain't had Indian trouble here in these parts for some time. The last time the Shoshoni *did* rise, they'd sort of outgrown bows and arrows in favor of Remington repeaters."

Longarm said, "I know. I got to swap shots with 'em down by the South Pass. I got the impression someone was trying to kill us discreet in that draw. They no-doubt have guns for more boisterous occasions. So I figure we ought to go back for the body with at least a dozen gunhands."

Haydock nodded. "I can round up more'n that, easy." Then he shot a more calculating look at his guest and asked, "Is it true you federal boys ain't allowed to put in for bounty money, even when you kill 'em your ownselves?"

Longarm nodded soberly. "It's a good way to get fired, whether it's lawsome or not. Am I correct in assuming Henderson had a lot of *dinero* posted on his fool head?"

"You are," Haycock said. "In his day, he managed to somehow offend everyone from the Cattleman's Protective Association to a couple of insurance companies and, of course, Carbon County just tossed five hundred in the pot for the killing of that deputy in Warren. So, seeing as I know where that draw is, and seeing as you can't claim part of the pot in any case—"

"You do the paperwork and he's all yours," Longarm cut in with a pleased expression. Then, as they shook on it, Longarm added, "Since Henderson's no good to me no more, I hope you won't mind my asking folk here in your town all sorts of fool questions. You know about the federal case I'm on, of course?"

Haydock nodded. "Yep. They keep sending us fliers about that missing greenhorn. His kin have posted a thousand-dollar reward for information leading to his rescue, recovery, or whatever. So I, for one, sure ain't sitting on no vital information. As far as I've been able to learn, asking my own fool questions, they never got this far."

Longarm pursed his lips. "Henderson said he met up with Johnny Two Hats here in town. That's *one* member of the party who made it, if Henderson wasn't making it up out of thin air entire. What do you think?"

Haydock shrugged. "It works both ways. This town ain't exactly Chicago, but it is the county seat. So a strange face can slip in and out easy enough. But if you're talking about a natural-looking breed, a prissy old dude, and a real-life black man riding into town aboard a red river cart, forget it. The boys as spit and whittle on the courthouse steps would never let a road show like *that* get by them, and we've asked 'em more than once whether they saw such a sight or not."

Longarm told the older lawman about the colored valet being left behind, sick, and asked for an educated guess on that. Haydock shifted his cud thoughtfully and opined, "The courthouse gang never seen no red river cart. Period. A couple of 'em are French Canucks and know what a red river cart looks like. As to a sick colored man bedded down within a day's ride of here, I fails to see how such a wonder could occur without us hearing about it. We got a lot more Indians than black folk in these parts, and we *try* to keep an eye on the *Indians*. There's been a roundup and many a Saturday night since that party was first reported lost out this way. Surely some cowhand riding in to get laid and drunk, in that order, would have mentioned that servant of the artist gent, if they'd heard tell of him."

Longarm sighed. "Well, I can't say I got the tale from honest men under oath, and whether Johnny Two hats was ever here or not, it hardly seems likely a local French Canuck would mistake a red river cart for a Conestoga wagon. Henderson said they met in some saloon, here, and that he thought the mastermind who wanted me dead might hang out there. I'm open to suggestions about said saloon."

Haydock shrugged. "This is neither a one-horse nor a one-saloon town, Longarm. You'll find eight licensed houses and a couple of shacks near the tracks as sell jars of white lightning when they think we ain't looking. There are more dumb fights in the Texas Queen than any other. So that would have been

115

a *dumb* place for Johnny Two Hats to hold secret meetings with anyone mysterious."

Longarm said, "That still leaves seven. Since Two Hats was a breed and I just come close to catching an arrow with my shoulder blades, where would I be most likely to drink in this town if I wore a feather in my hatband?"

Haydock shook his head. "Nowheres. Wyoming is still a territory, run federal, and serving Indians is a federal offence. I ain't saying a breed or even a sedate-dressed fullblood would find it impossible to buy a drink around here. But he'd surely have to leave his bow and arrows somewhere else and act more natural."

"Where would you say a well-behaving stranger could sip cider in a corner without drawing much notice as a stranger in town?" Longarm tried.

Haydock thought and said, "The taproom of the hotel, across from the railroad stop. Lots of strangers just passing through stay there and nobody pays 'em much mind as long as they don't act up."

Longarm thanked him for his advice, picked up his Winchester and possibles, and left to find the Majestic Hotel. He had to stay somewhere in town, in any case, and it was easy enough to find. Despite Old Haydock's brag, Basin was one hell of a lot smaller than Chicago.

The Majestic Hotel turned out to be a fair-sized two-story building trying to look like it rose taller behind its false front. The lobby had a pressed tin ceiling and some India rubber plants set in pots as if to shade the overstuffed chairs and brass spittoons scattered across what appeared at first to be Persian carpeting until Longarm noticed it had been painted on the pine planking, sort of cleverly. The wooden counter a snooty-looking clerk presided over had been painted to look like marble. Longarm went over to it and said he'd like a corner room in case it got any hotter. The snooty bird behind the desk sniffed and said he would no doubt feel more at home if he checked into the Drover's Rest across the tracks.

Longarm said, "I can pay in advance and I mean to shave any time now, Mr. Vanderbilt. Before this conversation gets any sillier, I'd best advice you I'm a federal government official—or a deputy marshal, anyways—and I still want a corner room."

The clerk gave him one, and allowed it was worth a dollar a night. Longarm said he doubted it, but paid for the key and said he wanted to leave his gear upstairs for now. The clerk tinkled a bitty bell and a colored boy came out of a rubber tree jungle in one corner to carry Longarm's bedroll and saddle bags. Longarm wouldn't give him the Winchester.

When the young fellow showed Longarm to his corner room and looked pleased about the dime he got for his hard day on the stairs, Longarm told him, "I got a question to ask a man of your complexion. I'm a lawman who's looking for an older gentleman of color in order to help him, not arrest him. Are you with me so far?"

The boy stared blankly up at him. So he tried, "The man's name is James. James Curtis, I think. He's a valet or house servant, traveling with his white boss, who'd be a white man with a spade beard, about fifty-odd. I'm not out to arrest him, either. I was told this James took sick on the trail and may be bedded down somewhere in these parts. How are we doing so far?"

The bellhop shrugged. "I ain't heard nothing 'bout no quality colored gent here, sick or otherwise, suh."

"Would you be likely to, if he was in town?"

"I 'spect I would, suh. They ain't but three colored families in the whole Basin and one of 'em's mine. I don't remember much about the War, and my

117

folk was free before then in any case. But they don't let us stay any old place in these parts, anyways. Be you colored, you's supposed to be in Niggertown, on the far side of the stockpens, after dark. That's what they call it, Niggertown, even if it only be a couple of houses and a barn."

Longarm nodded understandingly and said, "Well, the War was less than twenty years ago, and things keep getting better. You did say *three* colored families, didn't you?"

"Yessuh. Mine, the Jenkinses, and the Bronsons, just out of town. They raises pigs. The colored man you're looking for ain't there, neither. I know because me and Milly Bronson has us an understanding. I was on her porch swing with her just last night."

Longarm reached in his pocket again as he nodded and said, "I reckon it's safe to say the local colored folk ain't nursing him back to health, then. Do you think any of your kith and kin would have heard if he was, say, at any other local spread that might raise pigs, cows, or whatever?"

The boy seemed sincere as he assured Longarm that sounded sort of unusual, adding, "Most of the white folk in these parts is Southerners, suh. They might take care of one of their *own* niggers if they was allowed to keep niggers, now. I just can't see 'em treating some strange house nigger as a guest for any time at all."

Longarm handed him an extra quarter and told him it was to buy flowers for his Miss Milly. From the way the boy thanked him, he felt sure he'd hear about it if anyone else in the local colored community had any information about the missing valet. It was even safer to assume James Curtis couldn't be staying with any whites close enough to matter, unless small-town gossip just hadn't made it into the Basin with the rest of civilization.

He went back downstairs and checked out the taproom. It could be entered from either the lobby or by way of batwings facing the street. Either way, there didn't seem to be much going on at this hour. An upright piano stood silently against a back wall. There was a huge lithograph depicting Custer's Last Stand above the bar. Longarm found it sort of hard to believe the Indians had carried Zulu shields that afternoon, or that anyone could look so calm and noble in such a fix. But no doubt there'd been that much total confusion in the Little Bighorn at the time. So Longarm didn't try to figure it out any further as he ordered Maryland rye with a beer chaser.

The portly, balding barkeep said, "I notice you admire our picture of what took place not far from here," as he filled Longarm's order. Longarm was too polite to say he had just come down from the battlefield and that for openers not even the landscape had looked like that. The barkeep confided, "We may have more Indian trouble this summer. Some of the boys was just saying a white man got arrowed up the tracks near Bad Draw. Posse just rid out to see how bad things might be."

Longarm polished off the shot and washed it down quick before he replied, "I was wondering why business was so slow and, no offense, but that wasn't Maryland rye."

"Do tell? It sure says so on the label. We ain't never had no complaints about our liquor before."

"Just don't do that again and I won't have to call you a liar, then. I know I looks sort of cow as well as dusty. But I still ordered Maryland rye, and that wasn't even trade whiskey."

The barkeep eyed Longarm warily as a bigger and tougher-looking gent who'd been sort of dozing in a far corner slowly got up, or uncoiled, and moseyed over to join them, asking in a moody tone, "Having trouble, Morris?"

The barkeep smiled fondly at Longarm and said, "I ain't sure. This cowboy just intimated there was something wrong with our booze. But I feel sure he was only funning."

The fancier-dressed but rougher-looking moose on Longarm's side of the bar smiled wolfishly at him to purr, "Sure he was. Tell Morris you was only funning. It's getting too hot to fight in here."

Longarm stepped sideways from the bar, letting his coattails clear his cross-draw holster, and said, "You're right. I come in here for refreshment and mayhaps calm conversation, not for exercise. So now I want you to go right back to your corner and set yourself back down like a good little boy. Hear?"

It might have gone any way from there had not the barkeep been wiser as well as older than his backup. He said, "I think the man means it, Casey. There are times it makes more sense to serve a stranger what he ordered, and this could be such a time."

Casey growled, "Shit, I ain't scared of nobody, Morris."

The barkeep said, "I know. That's why I hired you. It was my mistake and I'll deal with it." Then he turned back to Longarm and asked, "Would you mind my setting up drinks on the house for the three of us if I somehow managed to find some rye?"

Longarm smiled thinly and allowed that was the best offer he'd had all day. As Morris poured, he held out his hand to Casey and introduced himself. The bully paled but managed a sick grin as it sank in. He said, "I'm sure glad I went to mass last Easter. For I see the saints was looking out for me today. But do we have to tell the world you crawfished me, Longarm? I got my own rep to consider."

Longarm raised his shot glass and said, "I didn't see nobody crawfishing around here. Business is business and social is social, right?"

So they clinked on it and, if the results weren't Maryland rye, Longarm had to allow it was whiskey, at least. He bought the next round and said, "I am reaching under my coat friendly because I want to show you boys some pictures."

As he spread some of the clearer prints from his dossier on the missing artist and his kith and kin on the bar, Casey looked disappointed and said, "Hell, I thought you had some hot French stuff. Who might them folk be, Longarm?"

The tall deputy said, "The middle-aged gent with the spade beard is a man I'm looking for, friendly. The dark-haired gal is his daughter, Miss Mary Lou Windsor. The colored gent is his valet or *segundo*. I don't suppose any of 'em have been in here or staying at the hotel, to your knowledge?"

The barkeep held a couple of prints up to the light to study better before he shook his head. "Nope. Wouldn't have served the gal or the nigger at this bar, in any case. I'd recall a gent wearing such a snooty beard and expression. I don't. So it's safe to say he ain't never been by."

Casey chimed in, "That pretty gal would be famous in Basin by now if *she'd* ever passed through. She's a real looker. How come you're more interested in her old man, Longarm?"

Longarm grimaced. "*She* ain't missing. She's the one as asked us to find her father, and I'm getting sort of tired of searching for the cuss."

Casey said, "Well, they do say you always get your man."

Longarm muttered, "It's the Mounties as make that brag, and they miss out now and again. Don't let this get around, but I don't know where Frank and

121

Jesse James are hiding out this summer and Clay County, Missouri, ain't as big as the Bighorn Basin. I'd have given up by now if I suspected Windsor had just fallen down a prairie-dog hole or got eaten by wolves."

"How do you know he ain't?" asked the barkeep.

Longarm told them, "Someone keeps trying to make me stop looking. Neither prairie dogs nor wolves have hired guns working for 'em."

The barkeep gulped and said, "Jesus, I surely hope no such cuss comes in *here* after you. For, no matter which way it turns out, it's a hell of a chore to bleach bloodstains out of pinewood flooring."

Longarm drained the last of his beer chaser. "I'd best go looking instead of waiting." He put his photographs away, said it had been nice talking to them, and left by the lobby entrance.

He decided his best next move would be to neaten up in order to avoid further discussions of his unkempt appearance. So he went upstairs to get his soap and shaving kit out. As he had almost made it to the door of his hired room, a door behind him opened and a voice called out, "Longarm?"

The big but fast-moving lawman crabbed sideways as far as he could get, which was the solid wall, and spun down and around to wind up on one knee with his revolver trained on the empty-handed as well as startled-looking gent standing midway down the hall in the light of a doorway.

As Longarm rose, lowering the muzzle more politely, he said, "I can see by your outfit that you ain't familiar with the customs of these parts. Now that you are, I hope you'll never call a man from close behind when he's on the prod again."

The stranger said, "For Pete's sake, I only asked the desk to ring me as soon as you came back to the hotel. I didn't know you were such a nervous type."

"I didn't know they had them newfangled Bell telephones in this hotel, either," Longarm said. "I got a right to be nervous. Would you like to tell me who you might be and what you might want with me, or am I just supposed to guess?"

The dapperly dressed and somewhat older man replied, "Oh, I'm sorry. I thought your offices wired you that I was on my way up from Denver. They said they would. I'm Cedric Smithers, Maxwell Windsor's art agent. No doubt you've heard of me?"

Longarm holstered his gun as he replied, "Not hardly. I ain't been by the Western Union yet. Let's get out of this hall one way or the other. Your room or mine?"

Smithers led him into his own digs. The air smelled like someone had been burning violets. Longarm wondered if the man used perfume or smoked fancy French cigarettes. In the better light from the open window, the dude's frock coat looked as much a dull shade of lavender as the light brown Longarm had first taken it to be, and he had a posy in his lapel only a shade more buttercup than his high-buttoned shoes. The artistic cuss looked a shade too old to have such shoe-black hair, naturally, and his small moustache looked as if he'd drawn it across his upper lip with one of the pencils fancy gals used to make their eyes look friendlier.

Smithers waved Longarm to a seat on the bed as he poured malt liquor into a couple of hotel tumblers, saying, "Miss Windsor got a rather disturbing communication from her father's darky just a few days ago. She insisted on coming west, so . . ."

"Mary Lou Windsor's here in Basin, too?" Longarm asked.

Smithers handed him his drink and replied, "Denver. I got her to stay *there*, at least, with a promise to send for her should I discover anything up

123

here. Good Lord, this is hardly any place for a lady, and they tell me it's the best hotel in town."

Longarm sipped his drink and forgave the flower in the buttonhole. At least Smithers *drank* like a real man. Longarm said "Good stuff. You say James Curtis wrote a letter to his employer's daughter?"

Smithers nodded and sat down on a bentwood chair near the bed as he explained, "In pencil, on brown wrapping paper. I wanted to bring it up from Denver with me, but your boss, Marshal Vail, told us it was evidence, and put it in his file on poor Maxwell. It would seem to indicate that James is being held at some ranch against his will. He said he was going to get a Mexican cowboy to post it for him. The handwriting on the envelope was in another hand and, if anything more illiterate. But, as we see it— and your Marshal Vail agrees—James came down with the ague on the trail. Miss Mary Lou says he's suffered from the recurring fever since his youth in the deep South. Maxwell left him with some rancher somewhere this side of the Crow Indian Agency, and naturally promised to pay for his servant's keep—by money order, one assumes—as soon as James was fit to travel on and catch up with him. As near as we can tell from the poor old darky's hasty scrawl, they're still waiting, and they won't let him go until they've been paid thirty-seven dollars. Have you ever heard of such a ridiculous ransom demand?"

Longarm grimaced. "They must have agreed on about a dollar a day for his keep, and a dollar is a lot of money to a hardscrabble spread. But since they ain't asking all that much it might make more sense just to pay 'em. Who's holding him, and where?"

Smithers sighed and said, "That's what driving poor Mary Lou so wild right now. There wasn't any indication where her father meant to meet James later. He neglected to include any return address in his hasty note. He probably told the Mexican who agreed to sneak it to the nearest postal drop for him that it was customary to put a return address on the envelope. There wasn't any. Your Marshal Vail thinks the cowboy just tucked the brown paper distress call in his vest and posted it in the white envelope when he got to he next town. There may have been a bit of a communications gap between James and his helpful cowboy. Mary Lou feels sure James speaks no Spanish."

"What about the postmark on the envelope? Even a dumb Mex had to send it stamped and postmarked, if it ever got all the way back East."

Smithers looked blank. Longarm muttered, "Old Billy's gotten fat as a hog behind his fool desk, and he still expects *me* to do all his paperwork for him. Never mind. I can get that from Denver by wire."

Smithers asked why it was so important. Longarm explained, "If you just come up from talking to Billy Vail in Denver, you likely know I traced Windsor and his valet, alive and well, as far as Hillsboro, Montana Territory. There ain't all that many places to buy a stamp between here and there. Mex cowhands are sort of rare, this far north, as well. If he was decent enough to post that letter for the captured colored man, he'd surely be willing to tell us where they was holding him."

Longarm shot a wistful glance at the oak and hard-rubber telephone set on the nearby bed table and added, "I can't wait until they get them things worked out to where a lawman will be able to talk from town to town. Crooks will be in a hell of a mess, and we won't have to spend so much time in telegraph offices."

Smithers asked, "Couldn't we just send telegrams to all the post offices between here and Hillsboro?"

Longarm shrugged. "We not only could, we *got*

to. But unless we get lucky as hell, the odds are that the Mex just bought himself a stamp at some cross-roads general store and dropped the letter in the near-est mailbox, sneaky. He must have known it was a secret message. He's more likely to tell the law than the world in general about a man that for all we know could be in the clutches of his own boss, see?"

Smithers grimaced. "You're right. People who want to be rescued really ought to include a return address. But even when you find James, and I'm sure you shall, what could *he* tell us about the more important matter of Maxwell's present where-abouts?"

Longarm shrugged. "For openers, James has to be this side of Hillsboro. That has to put us closer to where your client walked around the horses."

"Walked around the *what?*"

"Horses. This whole case is starting to remind me of a well-known and never-solved mystery. It hap-pened over in France a few years back, but sooner or later every lawman who reads up on famous cases frets himself to sleep about it. It's my own consid-ered opinion that the French lawmen who investi-gated the mystery missed something that might be more obvious if only it was in their fool published account."

He could see the agent was interested. So he sipped some more malt liquor and continued, "Keep-ing it simple, one day a French official was traveling from point A to point B in France aboard a mail coach. The French police made sure, later, that the coach crew and other passengers was all decent enough folk with neither criminal records nor pre-vious acquaintance with the official riding in their company. The coach stopped at a wayside inn and everybody climbed out to stretch their legs, take a leak, or whatever. Most of 'em naturally got out the

126

side facing the inn. The official got out the other side—facing an open fallow field on the far side of the road, by the way—and was last seen by one of the coach crew walking around the horses to join his fellow travelers. Ain't that a bitch?"

Smithers looked blank and asked what was a bitch. So Longarm said, "That's all she wrote. The man was never seen again. The coach couldn't leave without him. So he got searched for high and searched for low, even before someone called the law. He wasn't anywhere around that inn. He wasn't anywhere in or about the coach. He sure as hell wasn't on the open roadway or picking daisies in the meadow on the far side. The nearest cover was a quarter of a mile beyond, and nobody'd seen him headed that way to begin with. He just stepped out of sight, walking around the horses; and then he wasn't nowhere to be found."

"You mean he simply vanished into thin air on an open road in broad daylight?"

"I mean that's what it *looked* like. Nobody can *really* vanish into thin air. It wouldn't be natural."

"Then what do *you* think might have happened to him, Longarm?"

"I've no idea. I wasn't there. If I had been on that case I might or might not have spotted something them other lawmen missed. They spent a lot of time trying to scout up some play-pretty he might have wanted to run off with. When it turned out he was a happily married family man who didn't fool around on the side, they worked on the angle that he was working for the government and might have been packing secret papers and such. But they run that into the ground to no avail. They pestered all the man's known friends and enemies, questioned hell out of every possible witness to that last walk he took around the horses, and to this day no lawman has even come up with a sensible guess as to what might have really happened." He took another sip and added, "Sloppy investigating, like I said."

Smithers asked if he thought he was really being fair to the French peace officers. Longarm insisted, "They screwed up. They missed something. Since it naturally never wound up in their report, there's no way the case can ever be solved now. But it just ain't possible for a human being to wink out like a candle flame. Whether he done it himself or whether it was done to him, he had to be removed from the scene as a solid object—assuming he was ever there at all."

Smithers frowned. "But you just said he was seen in front of that inn, walking around those horses."

Longarm shook his head. "No, I never. I said them French lawmen was *told* that was what happened. *I* never seen it. Neither did they. A gent in my business learns to his sorrow that witnesses recall things that never happened the way they think they might have. And sometimes people even *fib* a mite. So when I'm faced with the choice of believing something that just ain't possible, or suspecting it just never happened, I tend to go with my suspicions."

Smithers shot him a wary look. "In other words, you suspect that Maxwell Windsor never really disappeared at all?"

Longarm said, "Oh, he's disappeared, to the extent that I can't *find* him, I'll allow. But let's study on that. How much would you know about his personal life, seeing as you're in business with him and all, Mr. Smithers?"

The agent looked uncomfortable and replied, "Enough to say that what you suggest sounds mighty silly. It's true I've only represented him the last three years, since his original agent passed away. But I know Maxwell well enough to assure you he's a respectable widower, dedicated to his art, with a healthy bank account, and no reason to run off and *hide* from anyone, for heaven's sake!"

"The stuff they gave me on him said he was a widower whose only child lives with him. She'd have noticed if he had something going on with, say, one of his models, male or female, right?"

Smithers looked disgusted. "That's a horrid thing even to suggest about an older gentleman dedicated to his art. I'll allow the man may have some human needs. But he'd never be indiscreet enough to conduct even a secret affair with one of the young ladies who pose for him. As for young men, that's monstrous to suggest. He was happily married until his wife passed away five or six years ago, and—"

"How do you know?" Longarm cut in. "You say you just went to work for him three years ago. Did someone tell you how he got along with a lady who must have died before you got a chance to meet her?"

Smithers looked pained. "I don't *work for* my clients, I sell their paintings. I consider myself and I hope my clients consider me their social equal. I naturally find myself at their homes quite often, as a guest. I've spent many a pleasant evening at the Windsor home on Fifth Avenue and they've naturally mentioned past events to me as we dined or sat by many a fire in Maxwell's study. There's a portrait of Mary Lou's mother above the fireplace. She was very beautiful. She was drowned in a boating accident on Long Island Sound one summer. They both miss her terribly. Whether Maxwell has lovers or not, as you suggest, it could hardly be anything serious. Certainly no reason for an established artist to abandon his family, his home, and his life's work."

"Who does Miss Mary Lou fool around with?" asked Longarm.

This brought Smithers to his feet, gasping, "What

are you, some sort of degenerate? She's only a child, you uncouth lout!"

Longarm said, "Aw, sit down and talk sensible. How was I to know you was in love with her? I ain't out to gossip about anyone. I just got to cover every angle, and she ain't all that childish if she was fourteen or fifteen when that portrait stole in Denver was painted. If you say a nineteen- or twenty-year-old rich gal in New York City ain't got no gentleman callers pestering her, I'll take your word for it."

Smithers looked sheepish and decided, "You're as good as they said you were. I know I'm too old for the girl. I didn't think it showed. I guess you consider me a dirty old man, too."

Longarm shook his head. "I never call no man dirty until I catch him doing dirty. There's method in my madness, though. Next to money, there's nothing that seems to cause more crime than slap and tickle, or the hankering for some. It occurred to me that a beautiful rich gal, kept on a tight rein by a strict father, has been known in the past to excite a man or more. You'd know, of course, if any young man has suddenly come calling with flowers, books, and candy since Maxwell Windsor ain't been writing home too regular?"

Smithers said he knew for a fact that Mary Lou had been too upset by her father's disappearance to receive any visitors of either sex. Longarm asked who, in that case, might have been with her all those lonely evenings, and was assured the house on New York's most fashionable avenue was well staffed with old and trusted servants. Windsor had only brought his personal valet west with him.

Longarm rose, put the tumbler down on the bed table with one good sip still in it, and announced, "I'd best go look for him, then. I'm sorry if I poked my nose into your client's linen. I had to make sure it wasn't dirty linen. Nothing you've told me gives me any call to suspect the man of vanishing on purpose. Now I'd best clean my own dirty self up and get back to hunting for him."

Smithers rose too, saying, "Let me come along. I told Mary Lou I'd do my best to find out what's going on up here if she'd stay in Denver out of harm's way."

Longarm said, "I'll let you tag along to the Western Union if you want to wait downstairs. You'd best wait in the lobby. There's a cuss in the taproom who might not admire that flower in your lapel. Don't you have a more sensible outfit to wear, if you mean to tag along with me?"

Smithers said he guessed he could pick up some denims and a wider-brimmed hat if he had to. Longarm said, "You have to. I got enough to worry about without worrying about otherwise innocent cowhands who might want to make you dance just for the hell of it."

Chapter 11

When next they met that afternoon, Longarm looked somewhat neater and was smooth-shaven. He had to allow Smithers made more sense in a denim jacket, pants, and Stetson, even if he still had to walk about in yellow high-buttons. He noticed the agent now had a short-barreled Colt Detective .38 tucked into the top of his jeans. He didn't comment. It wasn't his own balls at risk, if the man was dumb enough to have a round in all six chambers.

They went to the telegraph office. Longarm found a couple of wires waiting for him. Neither told him a thing he didn't already know. He brought Billy Vail up to date with a longer night letter and told Smithers, "So far, nothing. Now I got to wire every fool post office in the basin about that Mexican. Grab a pencil and help. Just copy my first form and we'll send the same message to everyone."

Working side by side, they soon finished. But as they stepped back outside, the sun looked somewhat lower and a mess of riders seemed to be coming in. Longarm saw some of them dismounting to enter a saloon across the way. He told Smithers, "Let's stick to beer, and don't talk too much. No offense, but you talk sort of fancy, and them new duds don't really make you look like an old range rider."

They crossed over and, as Longarm had hoped, nobody paid them any mind as they ordered a draft within earshot but apart from the regulars at the bar. Most of them had just come back from the recovery of Scribe Henderson's body. Longarm was mildly surprised to hear the place described as "Bad Draw." But he didn't ask why. He knew that once he identified himself he would be drawn deeper into the conversation than he might want to get. One louder hand who sported an unusual vest over his faded hickory work shirt was proclaiming that while the late cattle thief had no doubt deserved a short trail and a long rope, the infernal Shosoni had had no right to treat even an indecent white man so indecent. He said, "We found him with his pants down."

The barkeep asked how they knew the deed had been done by Shoshoni. Another rider said, "The arrows was neither Crow nor Cheyenne, and what's left? Shoshoni don't set much store by medicine stripes on their arrow shafts. They just put a steel trade head at one end of the stick and some goose feathers at the other and let fly, the uncouth sons of bitches. They shot Henderson in the back. Tried to shoot the lawman with him in the back as well, according to Deputy Haydock, who led us out to Bad Draw. That arrow was still stuck in a cottonwood. Plain Shoshoni, like the one in Henderson."

Longarm nudged the Easterner beside him and muttered, "Do you know how to ride?" When Smithers asked what he thought they rode in New York, camels? Longarm said, "Slip over to the livery. Tell 'em I sent you and that you want the buckskin and the black mare, both stock-saddled. Then lead 'em back here, tether 'em out front, and let me know."

Smithers said, "I will if you'll tell me why."

Longarm said, "Keep your voice down. Study the vest that one with the scar on his face has on and tell me if you think I'm looking at what I think I'm looking at."

Smithers stared blankly, longer than Longarm found sensible, before he sucked in his breath and said, "Oh, that's a butler's livery vest! James *was* wearing a similar one the last time he served me at the Windsor home, months ago!"

"Get them ponies, sudden. There's no time to worry about the saddle gun I left back at the hotel. We got to follow that old boy from here to where he got himself such odd attire for a cowhand."

The dude eased away from the bar and out the batwings. His departure had not gone undetected by the keen-eyed barkeep. As he drifted Longarm's way with a worried expression, Longarm told him, "He'll be back, and I'm paying, in any case. As long as you're down this way, you may as well replace the two dead soldiers we got here."

The older man looked relieved, refilled the two skimpy glasses, and said, "That'll be another dime."

Longarm placed a quarter on the mahogany and said, "I feel sure you'll inform me when it's time to ante up some more. As you may have guessed, I'm new in these parts. How come they call that place they're jawing about Bad Draw? Did someone lose a showdown, that way, earlier?"

The now friendlier barkeep confided, "It's an Injun name, translated sensible, of course. They say years ago the Crow jumped a Shoshoni camp up yonder and wiped 'em out entire, men, women, and children. Our own kids used to be able to find skull bones and arrowheads up to Bad Draw. But that was

a Halloween or more ago. According to the Injuns—
and some of the kids, of course—you can still hear
the spooks of dead Shoshoni moaning along that
draw at night. Coyotes, if you ask me. Lots of
coyotes has followed the herds north since the buffalo and wolves got thinned out."

Longarm thanked him for his cheerful local le-
gend and the barkeep left him to rejoin the more
stimulating conversation up the other way.

Longarm tried to nurse his beer. It wasn't easy,
considering how little they served for a whole nickle
in the rustic clip joint. One of the other customers
was holding forth on the old Indian battle in Bad
Draw now, and to hear him tell the tale it sounded
more ferocious than Little Bighorn. Longarm was a
keen student of human nature, including his own, so
he studied back on how he'd felt about that cottonwood he'd been about to water just before someone
put an arrow into it. He decided the wooded draw
hadn't felt haunted to him simply because nobody
had ever *told* him it was haunted. He wondered if,
had he known in advance about all the pain and suf-
fering those same old trees had seen, he'd have felt
they seemed broody and too shady, like the trees
along the much better known Little Bighorn. Human
nature sure played funny tricks on a man. Up there
where Custer had died, Old Man Death still seemed
to be hanging about. Bad Draw had just seemed like
a handy place to take a leak. Yet, in the end, it had
turned out to be a lot more dangerous neck of woods.

Cedric Smithers eased back beside him to murmur, "The horses are out front, ready when you are."

Longarm said, "I'm more so than that cuss in the
striped vest. He looks like he means to drink and
brag all night here in town. I reckon he don't get a
chance to be so famous too often."

"What do we do, just wait him out?" asked the agent.

Longarm shook his head. "Not in a joint that asks five cents for a drop of beer. We'd best eat something before we do any serious riding, and there's always another way to skin the cat. Let's go."

Smithers followed him out, but asked, "Where can we eat and still keep an eye on that man wearing the livery vest belonging to poor old James?"

Longarm said, "Keep your shirt on. I just told you we didn't have to. Come on, there's a hash house over there by the Western Union. I'll show you how we do things sneaky."

They entered to find the small counter half-occupied by other hungry gents, this close to sundown. Longarm ordered eggs over chili for both of them, ignoring the stricken look the Easterner shot at him. As they took stools and waited, Longarm asked the cowhand nearest to him to pass the jar of red peppers his way. As the hand did so, politely enough, Longarm chuckled and said, "Thanks. It looks as if we'll have to carry old Crawford home, and I'm already too drunk to carry my ownself. We been sort of celebrating the events in Bad Draw. Was you out there with us this afternoon?"

The hand washed down some beans with coffee. "Nope. But I just heard about it. *Crawford,* you say you got to carry home? No offense, but I disremember anyone called Crawford in these parts."

"Well, by any name we got to get him home. Me and Spike, here, just went to work with old whatever. So I could be mixed up about his name. We just left him over to the saloon, getting even drunker than us. He's the skinny one with a scar down his right cheek and that fool stripey vest we tease him about."

The hand laughed and said, "You're right. You're drunk. That's old Nate Jukes you're talking about.

137

How on earth did you wind up thinking he could be named Crawford?"

Longarm grinned sheepishly. "You know, now that I study on it, the ramrod of the *last* place we worked was old Nate Crawford. I reckon one Nate resembles any other in my present condition."

The hand said, "You'd best order extra coffee with that chili. How long has you boys been riding for the Circle J? I don't recall seeing you in town afore."

Longarm repeated that he and the red-faced Smithers had just arrived. The hand seemed to take that at face value and got up to leave, allowing it had been a pleasure to meet up with them.

As he did so, Smithers let his breath out with a wheeze and muttered, "Of all the brazen, bare-faced liars!" Longarm shushed him. "Keep it down to a roar. I ain't hardly started yet." Then, as the bored-looking half-breed waitress shoved their plates in front of them, Longarm told her, "I was just telling my pard, here, how much you reminded me of Miss Lillian Russell, the famous actress." It didn't seem to upset her, even though she did say, "She's a redhead, and it's only fair to warn you I'm spoken for."

Longarm sighed and said, "Well, you can't win 'em all. Do you know a Mex *vaquero* named Hernan, rides for the Circle J?"

She said, "No. My lover is pure white as well as jealous."

Longarm said, "This just ain't my night. I wasn't asking about old Hernan to steal his gal from him. I owe him money from a game of stud he won before last payday. I've been looking to pay up. But nobody in town seems to know him. I don't even know where his spread might be."

She said, "Oh, that's easy. The Circle J is just a few miles south of town. You can't miss it. They got a buffalo skull with Circle J painted on it, hanging above their gate near the wagon trace. I don't see how you could have missed it."

"To tell the truth, I expected it to be *north* of town. I do recall that buffalo skull, now that you mention it. We'd best have som pie to go with this chili. What kind have you got, this evening?" Longarm asked.

She said they could have any kind of pie they wanted as long as it was apple, and turned to slice some for them. At his side, Smithers muttered, "Nice misdirection," and Longarm said, "A magician gal I met up at Pine Ridge taught me a *lot* of tricks. Let's eat and coffee down good. We won't be riding until after dark, now. And I've time to get my saddle gun as well."

They rode back to the hotel together and tethered their ponies out front. Longarm wasn't surprised to learn that the art agent had not seen fit to arm himself with anything more serious than that bitty .38 before heading out into the Bighorn Basin with a flower in his lapel. But the man seemed to be a quick learner, and Longarm had said he could tag along.

But when they entered the lobby an even fancier-dressed gal leaped out of a chair to run over to them, sobbing, "Oh, Cedric, I've been so worried about you, and . . . What on earth are you dressed like that for?"

The embarrassed agent introduced the pretty little brunette to Longarm, saying, "This is Mary Lou, and I swear I told her to wait for us in Denver, Longarm."

Longarm half-closed his eyes to squint down at her and say, "Your hair was a mite lighter when you was fourteen or so, ma'am, but your dad sure paints good, albeit sort of fuzzy."

She asked, "Have you found my father? What about poor old James?"

Smithers told her, "We were just about to go looking for the darky. Longarm, here, thinks he knows where they've been holding him."

She said, "Oh, good! I'm going with you!"

Longarm said, "Not in that outfit, or even in wool chaps, missy. How come my boss, Marshal Vail, let you head up this way on your own?"

She dimpled up at him. "I didn't tell him or the deputy he had hanging about my hotel lobby I was leaving. I was going out of my mind, moping about down there with no news at all about my poor father or poor James. So here I am."

Longarm nodded and said, "And here you'll stay, then. You check her in whilst I go up and get my Winchester, Smithers. We can argue about it later."

He went up, got his saddle gun and some extra smokes, and when he got back down they were still arguing. Longarm told Smithers, "I'm holding you to keeping her here. If my suspicions was right about that cowhand's vest, I ought to be back here before midnight with the colored gent. If I was wrong, it won't take me that long."

Smithers asked, "Don't you think it could be risky going after James alone?"

Longarm said, "They've only been demanding thirty-seven dollars for his freedom, and I can manage *that*."

The girl stamped her foot and protested, "I don't see why I can't come along, in that case!"

Longarm told her, "The negotiations could get complicated enough without a pretty gal along to confuse a mess of unwashed horny gents, ma'am. You stay here with Mr. Smithers and, like I said, I'll bring old James back with me if he's there. I must say it will vex me, some, either way. For if your

140

father left him at a spread south of here, it means him and that breed must have gone even *deeper* into the Basin before whatever happened happened."

Smithers protested, "We've both asked here in town about that red river cart and nobody we've talked to seems to have seen it."

Longarm nodded grimly and said, "I was telling you before about how reliable witnesses can be. Meanwhile, James sure can't be checked into this hotel. So I'd best get cracking. Don't either of you try to follow me. I get broody at night when I notice anyone ghosting me in the dark. I mean that, Smithers."

The agent assured him they'd wait in town for him and he strode out to mount the black mare, telling her, "You'll make a worse target than me in the dark. We got us some night riding to do."

The Indian pony didn't argue. The moon was rising as they hit the south trail out of town and, though he reined in from time to time to cock an ear, they seemed to have the trail to themselves when he spotted the white buffalo skull staring down at them from its gate, just off to the west, and he turned in to see what happened next.

The first thing that happened was a yard dog barking fit to bust as Longarm topped a modest rise to spy it lunging all about on its chain, in the dooryard of a low-slung soddy with even more run-down-looking outbuildings around it. There was no sense trying to sneak into such a setup. He rode in boldly and as a front door opened he called out a howdy and just dismounted on the far side of the enraged dog as if he'd come to visit old friends.

The shabby-dressed, barefoot white gal in the doorway said, "There's nobody home. My menfolk rid into the county seat on business. It's only fair to warn you they'll be back any minute and my Nate is jealous-natured even when gents behave proper around me."

Longarm shooed her inside and followed, anyway, saying, "I was just talking to old Nate in town, Mrs. Jukes. We settled up about that colored gent, and I've come to fetch him, see?"

Indoors, in better light, she looked sort of pretty, or would have been, if she hadn't been frowning at him so suspiciously. She asked, "How could you have paid Nate for that nigger? Didn't he tell you we ain't *got* him no more?"

He said, "To tell the truth, your man was sort of drunk. The point is that this *is* the place a Mr. Windsor left his sick servant to recover, right?"

She shrugged and said, "He got well weeks ago. But they said they'd give us a dollar a day to tend him, and the nigger didn't have but nine dollars on him. Nate said he'd take that and a fancy vest he admired in part payment. But they still owed us thirty-seven dollars, and you got to get up *early* to slicker the likes of *us.*"

Longarm said, "I can tell you're smart, ma'am. Now I want you to tell me where James Curtis is."

"You'd best wait for my man and the others to get back. It ain't my place to discuss business with strangers."

Longarm said, "Oh, I should have introduced myself. My name is Custis Long and I'm the law, federal. I could arrest you and your husband for what's been going on here, but you just hand James Curtis over and we'll say no more about it."

She shook her head. "We ain't done nothing wrong. We nursed that nigger back to health under our very own roof and, by damn, we had a right to make an honest profit on his black hide!"

He sighed. "I can tell by your talk you're from the old South, ma'am. But the South lost, so the peculiar

142

institution is unlawful these days. Has been for some time. Whether you want to call it slavery or just plain kidnapping, you just can't hold a human being against his will, and I know for a fact that James Curtis would like to go home. So where is he?"

She looked away and said, "Lee may have surrendered. My Nate says *he* never, and that servant's *master* owes us *money*."

Longarm said, "All right. Take off your dress and let's see how good you screw, girl."

She turned pale as she could get under the dirt on her face and gasped, "Have you gone crazy? What gives you call to talk to me like that, you brute?"

He said, "Just playing by your own rules, missy. If you say the law of the land don't apply to you, and that you still admire slavery, I mean to treat you like my slave. I ain't got no cotton for you to chop, but that's all right. You're sort of pretty and I just feel like screwing you. So get out of them duds. That's an order."

"You crazy fool! My man will kill you sure as hell, now!"

He shrugged and said, "Maybe. On the other hand, by *his* rules, I got the right to kill him *and* screw you. As I see the peculiar institution, a man has the right to boss anyone around that he can boss, and I'm bigger and meaner than you *and* your man put together. So don't get uppity with your betters, gal. Shuck that dress and prepare to meet your maker."

She started to cry. He was glad she hadn't taken him up on it. He said, "It don't feel good when the shoe is on the other foot, does it? Do you want to cut this nonsense out and obey the law of the land, now?"

She sobbed, "We ain't got him no more. Nate sold

him to the Walkers. Miz Walker said she could use a house nigger and paid Nate forty dollars for him."

Longarm said, "I'm going to pretend I didn't hear that. Your man could wind up busting a heap of federal rocks for selling a man as a slave *this* long after Lee's surrender. You tell me where the Walker spread might be, and we'll say no more about it."

She shot him a cunning look and asked, "Will we have to give that money back?"

He said, "Not hardly. Nobody had any right to offer it for a human being. I don't see why I have to tell them *other* idjets just who told me *they* was holding a man in slavery illegal."

So in the end she gave him directions to the other spread, a good two hours' ride off to the west. As he was leaving she followed him outside to ask shyly, as he was mounting up, if he really thought she was pretty enough to enslave, if such wicked notions were still proper.

It would have been rude to tell her what he really thought of her unwashed charms, and she had been helpful, he hoped. So he ticked his hatbrim to her and told her with a gallant smile that it was no doubt fortunate for both of them that he was a lawman sworn to uphold the law of the land instead of a Viking, a Hun, or perhaps a Southern gentleman free to follow his own impulses about such matters.

Chapter 12

Lieutenant Colonel Austin Walker, late of the First
Texas Cavalry, C.S.A.—or so he said—had enjoyed
a grand late supper and was heeding the call of nature, out back, as he looked forward to the pleasures
of his sweet little Alda May's fourposter. But as he
opened the door of the privy and stepped out into his
moonlit rose garden, he saw he was not alone. He
frowned uncertainly at the tall, ominous shape loom-
ing above the path back to the house and said, "This
part of the grounds is off limits to the hired help,
son. Do I know you? I don't recall hiring a moose in
recent memory."

"I admire big outfits," Longarm said. "The dogs
don't bark when they're used to lots of smells coming and going. I took the liberty of waiting out here
for the inevitable because I was peeking through your
back window as you supped and, no offense, I have
discovered to my own chagrin that reed-slender gals
with big tits are inclined to be screamers."

The older man blanched, but had enough spunk to
declare, "You can have my wallet and a ten-minute
lead on my boys. But if you touch my Alda May I'll

kill you personal, bare-handed, and to hell with that bitty pistol in your hand!"

Longarm chuckled. "Don't get your bowels in an uproar. I ain't a robber. I'm the law, federal. I figure an outfit this imposing would require at least a thousand head grazing all about just to pay its grocery bills. Am I correct in also assuming you own clear title to no more than a quarter-section and such water as you found out here in the middle of nowhere much?"

Walker said, "I own half a section entire, and you insulted the size of my herd as well. What is all this about, son? Do you want to see my federal grazing permit? I got it in my desk in the house."

Longarm shook his head. "I feel sure you paid the Land Office the modest fee. My point is that no matter how any of us might feel about the surrender terms at Appomattox, the range you now enjoy so much belongs to the winning side. And, in this dog-eat-dog world, the winner gets to set the rules."

Walker shrugged and replied, "Hell, I had that figured out by the time I rid home from the War with no seat to my pants and a Yankee bullet in my leg. It still hurts when the weather gets damp. I tell you I've *paid* this year's grazing fees, and all my other papers is in order."

"I said I was sure they was. I've been given to understand you've been holding a colored man here in slavery, bondage, or whatever your defense lawyer aims to call it. Before you say you ain't, I feel it's only fair to repeat that I was watching you have dessert just now, and that didn't look like an Indian chief serving you and your wife."

The older man swore softly and muttered, "I told Alda May she could be a mite hasty in buying that nigger's debts from them trash whites over near the river. But that's all she ever done. You can't pin slave-raiding on us, damn it."

Longarm said, "I don't have to. Whatever the U.S. Government wants to call it, you'll sure play hell getting your grazing permit renewed next year if you're tied up in court as an unreconstructed rebel. On the other hand, I got more important chores to do, and I never was one for nit-picking paperwork. So why don't we just call old James out here and, if he doesn't want to press charges, we might be able to work this out to the advantage of both sides."

The old rebel hesitated, for while his Alda May was a mink in bed she could be a shrew at the breakfast table. But, as Longarm had assumed, he was a shrewd businessman. So he sighed and said, "You give me your word, as a man, that you'll just take the boy with you, quiet, and say no more about it, and we may have us a deal."

Longarm said, "I can't speak for James Curtis. He's a full-grown U. S. Citizen whose consititutional rights has been bent out of considerable shape. On the other hand, he may be anxious as me to get the hell out of here. And, oh, yeah, we'll need one of your ponies for him, saddled, and it might be best if you tagged along to give us your blessings until we're off the property."

"Damn it, son, that ain't much of a deal you're offering. For, aside from me winding up in the red for a horse and what we paid for the boy, my old woman is going to yell at me for weeks, if I get lucky."

Longarm said, "I could work it another way, if you like. I could just cuff you and take you back to town with me right now. Then I could come back with federal troops to rescue the slave noisy."

Walker gulped. "Well, since you put it that way, the boy is quartered just inside the kitchen door. But

147

what happens if he gets sassy and wants to press some fool charges, like you say?"

"When you make a bet you have to be ready to pay up when you lose. It would likely be a civil case instead of criminal if you can show in court you wasn't holding him all that tight against his will. So why don't you smarten up and quit holding him so tight?"

Walker nodded, led the way back to the house, and opened the back door to call out softly, "James? Get out here. I want to talk to you."

When the colored man came outside, he looked wary as well as old and weary. Walker said, "Boy, I want you to tell this lawman how well you've been treated and that we was only keeping you so's you could work off your just debts."

Longarm said, "Cut the bullshit and let's go find the man a mount. Evening, James. Your Miz Mary Lou sent me to fetch you. If you want this son of a bitch arrested, just say so."

The gray-haired James sobbed, "Oh, great day in the morning, I thought the South had riz again. But now all I want is to see that sweet child, Miz Mary Lou, again!"

A few minutes later Longarm and the rescued James were riding in the moonlight over rolling prairie. Then Longarm reined in, below the skyline, and when James asked why he said, "I aim to make sure that slavocrat is living up to his end of the deal. We're a long way from town, or even the river. It's no wonder you didn't know where they were holding you. How long has that been, by the way?"

James replied, "Over a month, at least. I come down with the ague after we got soaked in a spring rain, and Master Windsor had to leave me with those awful white trash. He promised them as well as me

148

that he'd come back for me in a week or so. But he never. How come he never come back for me, suh?"

Longarm told him gently, "He may not be alive, James. Thanks to our finding you, we know he made it at least this far south. But that's *all* we know for certain. You say you all got wet in a rainstorm. Does that mean you didn't still have that red river cart with you?"

James shook his head ."We had the cart, but it was too crowded under the canvas for all of us and all the gear my master brung along, and the canvas leaked, anyways. How come you want to know about that, suh?"

"Nobody saw you all after you passed through Hillsboro. How come? Wasn't you following the regular trail?"

"No, suh, that Johnny Two Hats convinced my master the landscape was more paintsome, did we follow old Indian trails he knew, a mite west of the regular one."

Longarm grimaced and said, "He sure was helpful. If he knew the country well enough to follow Indian trials through it, he had to know there was a colored community in Basin Township. So no doubt it was *his* notion to leave you with the trash whites at the Circle J, right?"

"He did say he knew they was decent folk, now that you ask. My master didn't know 'em, of course. But they acted all right until he went on with that half-breed boy. To tell the truth, that Mr. Nate Jukes didn't get ugly until two or three weeks went by and nobody come back for me."

Longarm said, "I reckon it's safe to ride on. I didn't think Walker wanted any more trouble."

Then, as they continued northeast at a walk, he said, "If your boss aimed to come back for you instead of sending for you, it means he'd seen about all he wanted of this basin and was fixing to turn back. Did they tell you where they was headed from the Jukes spread, James?"

The valet thought, nodded, and said, "Yessuh. It was Johnny Two Hats said it. My master didn't know the country. The half-breed boy said there was a grand view to paint at a place he called Leaning Rocks. He didn't say where it was or how far. But I got the notion it was on the east side of the Bighorn River. He said something about having to ford the cart across just north of some quicksand. That don't help, much, do it?"

Longarm smiled at him and said, "It might. You only get quicksand where a spring or a side branch stirs the bottom up, and Leaning Rocks sounds like a landmark well known enough to have its own name. We can ask about it in town, once we get you back there."

They rode in silence for a time. Then Longarm said, "I hope you won't take this wrong, James. But I can't help noticing you talk sort of Tidewater and still call your boss your master. Did you run off to New York State, before it was legal, I mean?"

James shook his head and said, "Master Maxwell took me. I was his personal slave when we was both much younger. He set me free as soon as we got up North. I reckon you could call him the white sheep of a fine old Virignia family. They disowned him, before the War, for his abolitionist notions. But he didn't need their money. He was a fine artist as well as a fine man. So he got rich all by himself, and never had to take advantage of other folks to do it. I stayed on as his body servant, even as a free man, because I still had to work for *someone*, and there wasn't nobody finer to work for, North or South, than Master Maxwell Windsor!"

Longarm got smokes out for both of them. As he

handed a cheroot to James, he said, "If you've been with him ever since he left all kith and kin behind in the tidewater country, you must have been there when he married a Long Island gal and they had Miss Mary Lou, right?"

James waited until he'd lit his own smoke before he told Longarm, "Miz Edith Ann was quality, too. As fine a lady as a fine man like him deserved. It like to broke my master's heart when she got drownded three or four summers ago."

"Well, he had his daughter to comfort him. What do you think of her, James?"

"Miz Mary Lou? Oh, she's a fine lady, too. I watched that child grow up. She's the only child they ever had. I'll allow she was bratty as most girl-childs, when she was little. But once she got full grown she took to acting ladylike as her poor mother. She's been a great comfort to the master since he's been alone."

"I heard she had no gentleman callers moping about to work up ulterior motives. What about the art agent, Cedric Smithers? He would have wound up with the job about the same time Mrs. Windsor wound up dead and their old agent died just as unexpected, right?"

James said, "Mr. Smithers seems a quality gentleman as far as I can tell. My job is to oversee the other servants, so I don't know anything about the art business. I do know Mr. Smithers got my master more money for his paintings than the *first* agent he had ever did. I know because I heard my master and Miz Mary Lou talking about it at table one evening. She was saying it was only natural that her father's paintings sold for more as he got older, better, and more famous. Master Maxwell never had as high an opinion of himself as others did. So he was a mite more pleased by the prices Mr. Smithers was getting for him."

"What kind of money are we talking about, James?"

"Oh, Lordy, I don't know nothing about such matters, suh. I recall whistling, some, the night Mr. Smithers come by to say he'd sold a landscape for more than a thousand dollars. But I ain't never been too good at numbers."

"Can you guess how many paintings they had in that red river cart the last time you looked?"

"Not exactly, suh. My master was a painting man. It must have been more than three dozen, though. I know we started out with four dozen empty canvases, and he was starting to worry about having enough by the time I come down with the ague. Do the exact numbers matter, suh?"

Longarm shook his head. "Not hardly. At no more than a hundred dollars a finished canvas—and I *know* they'd have to be worth more than that—we're talking thirty-sixty hundred dollars, and I know Johnny Two Hats was willing to gun a lawman for five hundred!"

Longarm had barely managed to keep his promise about midnight. But as he and James strode into the hotel lobby, a heavy-set gent who looked somehow familiar was pretending to read a newspaper in one corner. He refused to meet Longarm's eye. Longarm nodded to him, anyway, and waited until they were on the stairs before he asked James if he had ever seen the man before. The old valet sounded more saddle-sore than interested as he replied that he hadn't noticed the lobby lounger.

But the rescued servant perked up considerably when they got upstairs to find Mary Lou Windsor waiting in Smithers's room for them. She and the old colored gent hugged one another like father and daughter. Then she hugged Longarm for saving James, albeit not in a daughterly fashion.

That was fair. He didn't feel old enough to be her father, and she sure was padded nice. He told all three of them, "This hotel may or may not accept guests of James's complexion. But what they don't know can't upset 'em. He can bunk in my room, and I'll work something out once I get tired. I got to send some wires and ask more questions around town about local landmarks. James, here, has had a long ride as well as a rough day. So I want to put all three of you to bed. You'll have plenty of time to talk on the train back down to Denver."

Neither man seemed to want to argue. But Mary Lou told Longarm he was crazy and added that she had no intention of leaving without her dear father.

Longarm said, "You got to. The train I mean to put the three of you aboard pulls out just after eight in the morning, and I can't afford more time than that. I don't want to needlessly upset you, Miss Mary Lou. But things don't look good for your dad and, dead or alive, we're dealing with mighty dangerous folk, no matter what in thunder they're really up to."

Smithers frowned and asked, "Haven't you figured that out yet, even with James, here, to help you?"

Longarm shook his head. "Nope. All I know, now, is that your client walked around the horses after he left the Circle J just a few miles south of here. He may or may not have been headed for a place called Leaning Rocks. That's where I mean to look for him next. If I find him sitting there painting a landscape, I'll be surprised as well as vexed with him. But I got to look *some* infernal place. I look better when I only have to worry about my own back. That's why I mean to make sure the three of you are on your way down to Denver, with other deputies waiting to meet your train, before I ride out again."

Smithers said that made sense. James said nothing. Mary Lou stamped her foot. Longarm told James to come with him and led the weary old man to his own corner room. He lit the lamp and said, "There you go, James. You try to get a good night's sleep, and come this time tomorrow night it won't be as complicated. They provide servants' rooms at the Palace in Denver."

The old man said, "God bless you, suh. I don't know how I'll ever repay you for all you done for Miz Mary Lou and me."

Longarm said, "I get *paid* to act foolish. Hit the damn sack and I'll see you in the morning."

He stepped out in the hall and closed the door. As he did so, the next one down opened and Mary Lou stuck her head out. She said, "That was very generous of you, Custis. But I don't want you sleeping in the lobby or, even worse, with some woman of the town, as they call them in the Good Book."

He smiled down at her and said, "I hardy ever pay for bed pards, ma'am. What gives you the call to intimate I never sleep alone, in any case?"

She opened her door wider, letting him see that she'd shucked all but her shimmy shirt and silk stockings as she grinned back at him roguishly. "Anyone who sleeps alone when he or she doesn't *have* to is made of sterner stuff than *I* am, I fear."

He said, "I fail to see why you're teasing me like this, Miss Mary Lou. But if it's any comfort to you, it hurts like hell."

She asked him what made him think she was teasing. Then, as he herded her inside the dark but moonlit room and shut the door after them, she added uncertainly, "Weren't you going to run some errands first, Custis?"

He said, "I can't think of anything else I might want to do that can't wait until morning." Then he picked her up and carried her over to the bed.

She giggled and said, "Oh, I was afraid you'd never ask."

He lowered her to the mattress and proceeded to shuck his duds before she could change her mind. But she beat him to the buff, having nothing of her own to shuck but her shimmy. She left the stockings on. They looked wicked but felt sort of scratchy around his waist as he settled into her warm love nest and they both went crazy for a spell.

Later, when they paused to get their second winds, she said, "I hope I surprised you as pleasantly as you surprised me, dear. I knew you were tall, but not *that* tall. Is that why they call you Longarm?"

He chuckled. "I got the nickname reaching out for less beautiful critters. But you're right about my feeling mighty surprised. I've been told by two grown men that you was a daddy's girl who didn't have many gentleman callers."

She snuggled closer and said, "My father wouldn't have been too keen about me entertaining men at home like *this,* and neither James nor that stuffy old Cedric Smithers are my type."

He said, "I just gathered as much. From the way you move in bed, no offense, I'd say you have met more than one man in the past who did tickle your fancy, as fancy."

She said, "Don't be beastly. I've always been very discreet as well as choosy. Father never paid attention to my comings and goings, once he was locked up in his studio with his art and sometimes an artist's model. I suppose, if the truth would be known, all of

155

us artistic folk are free thinkers on the subject of sex. Can I get on top, now?"

She didn't wait for an answer. As she struck a mighty artistic nude pose in the moonlight Longarm laughed up at her and said, "I must be artistic, too. For you've got me inspired as hell. But I sure would have taken you for a proper home gal, with your duds on. You looked innocent as anything in that early portrait your dad done of you."

She moved amazingly, considering how calmly she could still talk as she told him, simply, "I *was* a good little girl when that picture was painted. I guess I went kind of crazy for a while when my mother died. I ran off with a male model, drank like a fish, and when my father finally found me I was in an awful state."

"I've noticed how wild some young gals can get without a mother riding herd on 'em. He took you back, just the same?"

She stopped moving on him as she almost sobbed, "He had to. He was that kind of man. I tried to make it to up to him by being the good daughter he and Mommy thought they'd raised. I think I *have* been good, save for this secret vice I've never managed to lose interest in. But why on earth am I telling you the story of my life now, for heaven's sake?"

Longarm didn't feel much like talking, either, by the time he wound up back on top with two pillows shoved under her. But once they'd come back down from the moon to lie panting in each other's arms, he found himself asking, "Have any of your other lovers ever tried to get you to marry up with them, so's they could be related to a famous artist?"

She said that was a silly question to ask any lady he was in bed with. So he said, "No, it ain't. More than one other gal has pointed out to me, with considerable annoyance, that under our present property laws a husband has the right to do whatever he likes with his wife's property, whether he gave it to her or whether she got it from her own kin."

She gasped and said, "My God, you *are* the long arm of the law, and I ought to feel insulted, considering the time and place you still seem to be conducting your investigation. But it is my poor father's property you're asking about, so, no, that won't work. It's true I've had lovers ask me to marry them. That's usually about the time I'm dropping them. I've never been seriously involved with any man since that first one I really loved tried to sell my body to feed his opium habit. It wouldn't do a man any good to murder the wealthy father of a girl who didn't want to marry him, would it?"

He said, "Not hardly, and I'm glad we can scratch that notion off. James tells me your dad had at least three dozen paintings with him when he vanished. There's that one someone stole from the Denver musuem, too, adding up to someone with a whole mess of signed originals. How hard would it be to peddle all that art work without you or your agent noticing, honey?"

She shrugged her naked shoulder against him. "We were talking about that while you were out looking for James. Cedric thinks it would be just about impossible as long as I was alive and he was my father's agent of record. That small portrait of me wouldn't be worth more than a few hundred dollars in the first place. The others couldn't be sold with Father's signature left on and, with the name of the artist *changed,* he thinks they'd only be worth what they looked like—paintings by some unknown artist in a style he'd copied from a master. No more than, say, ten or twenty dollars apiece."

He sighed and said, "That might be enough for one petty crook like Johnny Two Hats to kill for.

Hardly enough to inspire a master-mind paying for multiple crimes by a mess of sneaks."

"Do you really think they've done away with my poor father?" she sniffed.

He patted her bare rump reassuringly, but told her, "We got to consider it, like it or not. We got to consider that you and even Smithers could be in danger, as well. As I put it together, there's nobody else who could say, for sure, whether a Maxwell Windsor painting had been come by honestly or not."

She shuddered and said, "Oh, Lord, I never thought of that! Hold me, Custis. Touch me, naughty, and make me forget how cold and cruel the world can be outside your strong loving arms!"

He started to. Then they both stiffened as the night was rent by the sounds of gunshots and breaking glass!

She gasped, "What was that?" and he said, "It wasn't anyone shooting through your window at us. I'd best get dressed and gunned so's I can find out who *else* is in trouble!"

Chapter 13

The doorway of Longarm's corner room was crowded as he stood further inside, staring morosely down at the body of James Curtis. The old colored gent lay half dressed between the bed and one window with about as many bullets in him as there were in the drawn-down windowshade. The bedside lamp was still lit. It was easy enough to put it together. The valet had gotten up from the bed, perhaps to use the chamber pot, or for some other reason, and the lamp had cast his shadow against the shade for some some of a bitch outside to aim at.

The desk clerk from downstairs elbowed his way in to join Longarm and demand, "What happened? How come there's a dead nigger bleeding all over our rug?"

Longarm said, "They was more likely aiming at me. Is a heavy-set gent in a business suit still setting down in the lobby and, either way, who might he be?"

The clerk looked blank, gathered his wits back together, and said, "Oh, right, one of our guests *was* sitting down there up until a few mintutes ago. His name's Waxman and he's a whiskey drummer from Omaha, I think."

Longarm said, "Go get him, along with the town law. I'll trim this damn lamp so's we don't draw no more fire in the meantime!"

By this time Mary Lou had dressed as well and joined the crowd in the doorway. When she saw what had happened she sobbed and forced her way in to fall to her knees by the body to cry out, "Oh, my God, who could have wanted to harm poor old James?"

Longarm snuffed the lamp and raised the shade of another window to shed some safer light on the subject as he replied, "It couldn't have been you or me. After that it's up for grabs. But I suspicion they mistook his shadow against the shade for mine."

Cedric Smithers came in to ask, "What's going on? Who's that on the floor?"

Longarm told him, "James. He's dead. Where have *you* been all this time?"

Smithers said, "In the taproom downstairs. They just told us there'd been a shooting up here. I don't think I like the way you put that question, Longarm. What reason would *I* have for hurting the man?"

"It don't matter, seeing you got witnesses to prove you never. I don't think anyone was after him to begin with," Longarm said.

Deputy Haydock came in to ask what all the fuss was about. Then he spotted the body by moonlight and said, "Oh. It sure has gotten noisy since you showed up, Longarm. Why did you gun this one?"

"He was on my side," Longarm said. "Look at them bullet holes in the shade and the busted glass on the floor. His name was James Curtis. He was a servant of that artist gent I told you about."

Haydock hunkered down for a closer look before

he opined, "They sure done a job on him. Any notion why, or who?"

The room clerk came back to report the mysterious whiskey drummer was neither in his room nor in the lobby at the moment. Longarm told Haydock, "When we come in, say no more than an hour ago, a somehow familiar face was pretending to read a newspaper down in the lobby. I suspicion he was waiting there for someone and, while I'm sometimes wrong, I might have recalled his face from a rogues' gallery photograph I should have paid more mind to. Whether he's a hired gun or not, his alibi ain't as good as some others I seen around here this evening. So we'd best try to pick him up. We're looking for a gent about forty-five or fifty, heavy-set, smooth-shaven. Oh, yeah, the top parts of his chubby face was tanner than his jowls, so he may have shaved recent after coming in off the range less neat. He's dressed town, or was. I'll sure feel dumb if we find him at the bar downstairs."

"You won't," Smithers said. "The taproom wasn't crowded at this hour and I didn't see anyone fitting that description coming in or out."

Longarm nodded grimly. "Yep, it adds up to a stakeout, and I ought to be stood in a corner for not getting *that* answer off the blackboard."

Haydock stared soberly up at the perforated window-window shade and said, "He surely must have been paying attention to you, Longarm. There ain't no train out before morning and I got the manpower for another posse. But, I dunno, even with the moonball shining full, the earth's baked summer-hard."

Longarm said, "Don't waste time trying to cut his trail. It might make more sense to look for him here in town. He was checked in here. So he may have to hunt a spell for *other* cover."

Haydock rose. "That's saying he wasn't planning

on hiding nowheres until *after* he gunned a federal deputy smack in the center of town. If I was planning such a deed, I feel sure I'd have some escape route already worked out."

Longarm sighed. "So would I. He's likely back under some wet rock by now and we'll never catch him until he crawls out from under it again. But speaking of rocks, where would I be if I was called Leaning Rocks? Far side of the river?"

Haydock nodded and said, "That's easy. You just have to go on up to the next ford and there's a sign-post reading Cloud Mount Trail. You don't have to follow the trail that far, though. Leaning Rocks is a freakish outcrop leaning toward the crests of the Bighorns. Injuns used to use the Leaning Rocks as a hideout. Don't ask me why. You can see the land-mark for miles. What have the Leaning Rocks got to do with this colored gent, here?"

Longarm said, "He mentioned 'em to me earlier. I'd best ride yonder for a look-see, tomorrow, after I get some other likely targets safely off to Denver."

Mary Lou looked up from where she knelt with the dead man's head in her lap to protest, "I'm not leaving now, Custis. Not while you're so close to solving the mystery of my father's disappearance!"

He said, "Sure you are. I don't know how close I might be to solving anything, but anyone can see I've got someone else mighty nervous. I'm going to wire ahead. When you and Mr. Smithers get to Denver you'll find my pals waiting to see you both safely to the nearest decent hotel. I want you to wait there until you hear from me one way or the other. It won't be all that long. I'll pick up the trail at Leaning Rocks or I won't. If I don't, Billy Vail will likely tell me to pack it in, for now. With both the men who left the Crow Agency with your dad dead, the trail is getting cold indeed."

"If the trail's so *cold,* Longarm, how come some-one keeps trying so hard to keep you from *cutting* it?" Haydock asked.

Longarm shrugged and said, "Beats me. They must think I know more than I really do. I'll be switched with snakes if I can make head nor tail out of this mess."

Longarm made sure they got to the railroad platform early the next morning. Mary Lou still said she wanted to ride on to Leaning Rocks with him. But he'd calmed her nerves considerably with some early morning slap-and-tickle, and Smithers kept telling her not to be silly as well.

As they waited in the morning chill, near the mountain of baggage it took to move two Eastern folk about, Longarm consulted his pocketwatch, saw they still had twenty minutes to wait, and chose his words carefully as he asked the art agent, "Seeing as you'd know more than me about artistic estates, am I correct in assuming Miss Mary Lou, here, don't fig-ure to inherit much unless and until we can prove her father's no longer with us?"

She told him that was an awful thing to say. Smithers was a man, so he said, "Well, naturally, nobody would be in any position to dispute her rights to live in her own home until the probate court works something out one way or the other. As the agent of her father I still have the right to sell his paintings no matter what."

"Even if he's in no condition to bank the money?"

"Hmm. I suppose we would have to hold such money in escrow for Miss Mary Lou, here, until it can be established whether it's due Maxwell Windsor or his estate. Do we have to have this grim discus-sion, Longarm?"

The younger man said, "We do. Sorry, Miss Mary

163

Lou. It's crossed my mind that a rich man missing entire causes more vexation for his heirs—in this case only one—than if we was able to find him dead for certain."

Mary Lou looked as if she was fixing to cry. Smithers took one of her arms and soothed, "I think I see what he's getting at, dear heart. As ghastly as it may sound, you'd be the one person who'd have no motive to want your father's whereabouts, dead or alive, a mystery."

She dabbed at her eyes with a kerchief and may have been about to say something to Longarm. But then her eyes widened in sheer horror and she gasped, "Oh, no, don't!" as she stared past him at something or somebody else.

Longarm shoved the girl one way and spun the other as he whirled about, drawing his sixgun. There were two of them; the stubby one he'd seen in the hotel lobby and a taller one, dressed more cow. They were both slapping leather and Longarm saw, sickly, that he could only shoot one at a time. He fired at the heavy-set one. At the same time, another gun went off in his ear and the taller one folded like a jacknife over his gunbelt and flew backward off the platform.

Longarm turned to see Cedric Smithers, of all people, standing there with a bemused expression on his face and the dinky .38 still smoking in his hand. Mary Lou was on her sweet rump beyond the baggage and, bless her, she was still alive and well, too.

Longarm nodded and said, "I owe you. Where did you learn to handle a gun like that, old son?"

Smithers said, "I was a platoon leader in the New York Seventh Infantry. Didn't get in much pistol practice against Johnny Reb. But the New York draft riots were educational as well as house-to-house."

Longarm holstered his own gun. "We live and learn. Let's see who we just shot it out with."

As they reached the end of the platform half the town, led by Deputy Haydock, seemed to be coming to join them. The two bodies lay face-up in the grit off the end of the planking. Longarm stared soberly down and said, "Oh, the one dressed cow is easy. He used to be Dodge City Dillon. A noted backshooter who worked cheap. I could swear I'd seen that older one somewhere before, but I can't just place him."

Smithers gasped and said, "I think I can! He looks like an art dealer I've seen at more than one New York auction! I don't know his name, but it has to be him!"

Deputy Haydock joined them to ask, "What have we got here?"

Longarm said, "More bounty money, if you'd like to do the paperwork on Dodge City Dillon. He's the one in the denim shirt. Wells Fargo said he was worth five hundred to them, dead or alive, so his present condition doesn't matter. We're still working on the other one. I've been to New York City, but not to buy no artwork. My pard, here, thinks he could be an art dealer from back East. I'll be damned if I can say the same. He just looks like some damned body I've met before. Before last night at the hotel, I mean. I suspicion we just got the one who murdered James Curtis in my room."

Haydock said, "I sure admire a man who keeps things so simple for our coroner. But you did mention something about reward money just now, didn't you?"

Longarm spotted locomotive smoke to the north as he replied, "I did. It's a good thing you got the sons of bitches. My friends, here, have a train to catch. Smithers, why don't you go help Miss Mary Lou up and get her aboard? I'll tidy up here and we'll talk about estates and such when I join you in Denver."

That was how they worked it out. Before noon, Longarm was on his way to Leaning Rocks, wondering if he was alone on the trail or not. If he wasn't, the gang had to be so big that art theft just wouldn't work as their motive.

Chapter 14

Johnny Two Hats had been telling the truth about quicksand, at least. When Longarm got to the ford he found a warning sign nailed to the post the larger trail arrow was mounted on. But as he forded the river, riding the buckskin and leading the black, he didn't run into any, and the water was so low he didn't even wet his boot heels.

The Cloud Mount Trail on the far side was a two-rut wagon trace, near the river, at least. But summer-killed weeds he saw scattered along both ruts told him nobody used the trail much these days. It had likely been blazed by Indian traders a few years back, when there were still enough Indians in the Bighorns to make trading with them worth the effort.

Like most such trails, it followed the easy grade, twisting and turning to avoid high ground. Longarm rode a more direct route, keeping the trail in sight most of the time but cutting across the draws and rises of the rolling range east of the river. He reined in now and again on a rise to look back, of course. But nobody seemed to be ghosting him, and after the first few miles it got even more unlikely. For the ground was getting even higher as he approached the more serious foothills of the Bighorn Range, and he could see all the way back to the riverside flats by now.

Then they were in ever-thickening timber and he couldn't see backward or forward enough to matter. He drew his saddle gun, levered a round in its chamber, and rode with it across his thighs a spell. He had to follow the trail now. It took him around a bend to where the two ruts turned into one narrow pony trail. The old-timers had obviously found it unprofitable to haul anything on wheels higher up the considerable slope. So Longarm wasn't surprised to see signs of many a campfire. Most were just ash heaps flattened and spread by more than one good rain but betrayed by the fireweed that gave their scattered locations away. Regular shortgrass was growing where it could. A fresher big pile of ash and charcoal was still bare against an outcrop of rock about thirty yards off the trail. The rock rising above the pile was smoke-blackened, and Longarm muttered, "Wasteful and careless, even for white men. Good thing they had enough sense to build it against a natural fireplace. These old pines all around burn mighty hot as well as easy."

He rode on up the narrower pony trail. He hadn't gone a mile when he spotted the Leaning Rocks. They were off the trail and upslope from the pony trail, which just kept going. But there was no mistaking the landmark. It looked as if some gigantic kid had used giant slabs of sandstone to build one of those houses kids build with playing cards by leaning them together.

He dismounted and tethered his ponies to an aspen by the trail to move on up on foot, Winchester at port.

But when he got there, there was nothing there.

Streaks of soot showed him the natural rock shelter had been used in the past as a dry campsite. But there was no sign to read in the birdcage gravel and bits of charcoal forming the current floor of the shallow shelter. Some earlier hand had scratched through the soot above to leave his initials and the date, 1868. Longarm grimaced and muttered, "That don't work for anyone I'm interested in *this* summer." But he hunkered down with the Winchester across his thighs and poked about in the dust and gravel anyway. All he got for his pains was some busted bottle glass, a flint arrowhead, and what he hoped wasn't really a lump of mummified shit.

He rose and went back to his ponies. As he swapped saddles for the ride back to town he told the ponies he was sorry for bringing them all this way on a fool's errand. "They never could have got this far with that red river cart, anyway. James got it wrong or, more likely, someone was fibbing. There's a lot of that going around up this way."

Riding the black pony and leading the buckskin, he made better time moving downslope than up. When they got back to where the trail was two ruts again, he reined in, dismounted, and moved over to the remains of that bigger campfire.

It hadn't been a campfire. Campers had been known to toss a loose shoe nail into the fire now and again, but when Longarm spied dozens of rusty red little nails winking up at him from the big pile of ash an charcoal he leaned his Winchester against the rocks and hunkered down to commence sifting through the ashes with his fingers.

There were even more of the short, sharp nails than met the eye. The ones deeper in the ash weren't rusted, although they were fire-gray. He held one up to the light. It had to be one of those bitty nails that hold an artist's canvas tight on its wooden frame. He found some buttons and a shirt stud. Then his questing fingers encountered a length of thin chain. When he tugged on it, he pulled out a plum indeed. It was a man's pocketwatch, expensive, though the fire had played hell with its gold finish. Longarm opened the case. The gold was still shiny inside. It was easy to read the engraved inscription. "To Maxwell Windsor from his sometimes naughty but ever loving Mary Lou."

Longarm sighed, stood up, and went back to the ponies to break out a spade from his packsaddle. He could see that he had some serious digging to do, now.

The smaller bones had been consumed by the fire. But wood just didn't burn hot enough to cremate the pelvic, spinal, and long bones of a human being. He found the skull almost intact. As he placed it gently on a tarp along with the other evidence, he told it, "Well, old son, I can't say it's a pleasure meeting you like this. But, to tell the truth, I was getting mighty tired of searching for you."

Later that afternoon Longarm had just finished laying out all his material evidence on the long trestle table the township of Basin had provided him, in the cellar of the town hall, when Deputy Haydock came in to join him with the somewhat bemused townfolk he had rounded up. As they gathered around the table, the only woman in the group, a little sparrow bird of a schoolmarm, looked dismayed by the skull grinning up at her from one end of the table. Longarm told her, "Miss Compten, I set up the arrows I want *you* to look over down at the far end. I'd like whichever one of you is the dentist to work on that skull for me."

As the little schoolmarm gratefully changed places with the confused local dentist, Longarm said, "I'd

170

like Mr. Fong to move there, and Mr. Feldman gets to examine that watch next to the linen. Which one of you might be Mr. Davis from the photographic studio?"

A younger youth than Longarm might have chosen as an expert raised his hand. When Longarm asked if it was true he did photo retouching, David nodded. Longarm said,"You'd best come around on this side, then."

Once he had his volunteers sorted out, Longarm said, "All right. For openers, I want to thank you all for coming here today, whether we figure things out right or not. I have to tell you before I take up any more of your time that, much as I'd like to, I can't pay you for your time. Any questions about that?"

The middle-aged jeweler, Feldman, said, "Deputy Haydock just explained that the law needed our professional help, and of course it's our duty to help the law. But none of us have any experience as police investigators."

Miss Compten chirped, "Aaron is right. I'm a school teacher, for heaven's sake!"

Longarm said, "I know that, ma'am. They tell me you're also interested in Indian culture and that you've been collecting baskets, blankets, and such since you came out here from the East a spell back. I know none of you have ever worked on criminal evidence before. That's why I called on your individual expert help. For I work for the law all the time, and I've been stumped by some mighty sneaky goings-on. It's my hope that eyes with a fresher point of view and mayhaps keener vision for the details of each one's chosen craft might be able to help me put this puzzle together. You'll note I've written what I want each of you to look for on them slips of paper by each item of evidence. I don't want you comparing notes, for the same reason I ain't told you a thing

171

about this case except that it's a serious crime. I got to go send some wires, now. Feel free to work on the chores I've given each of you here or, if you'd rather, feel free to take 'em home with you. Either way, let's all meet here again this evening after supper. Say seven o'clock?"

There was murmur of agreement. But the little schoolmarm held up one of the arrows from Bad Draw and said firmly. "I can tell you here and now this is not an Indian arrow. It's from a machine-made archery set. I know because when I was at Vassar I was on the archery team."

Longarm smiled at her and said, "There you go. I suspected as much. But now I can say for sure. Why don't you just study them arrows some more and tell me, after supper, what else you may be able to figure out from them?"

Fong, the laundry man, held up the shirt the mysterious gent Smithers thought was an art dealer had been wearing when he died and asked sort of timidly, "How me gonna tell Chinee laundly this man take shirtee fow washee, my word? This shirtee need lotta washee to get blood out and I see son of Han's laundly mark on he colla! But Fong no savvy otha' laundly man's name. He no put he *own* name on shirtee. Just put mark of man who *wear* he!"

Some of the others laughed at the man's funny way of talking. Longarm nodded at him soberly and said, "If you'd read your own instructions again, sir, you'll see that while the dead gunslick was packing a mess of business cards with different phony names on them, the labels inside his duds showed everything he had on had been bought in New York City. I'm sure I've seen him somewhere closer. But a pal of mine made him out a New Yorker as well. So it stands to reason he had his laundry done there. I'm glad you agree them laundry marks was made by some gent of your own persuasion. If you can figure out how to narrow it down some more, I can wire some New York detectives I've worked with in the past to narrow it down even more. If they could locate the New York laundry, the laundry would surely know who it did shirts and underwear for, see?"

Fong said he had to go home and study some Chinese books. As he left, the jeweler held up the charred watch and said, "Me, too. This is a fine timepiece. You don't buy a watch like this just anywhere. Also, it's got a serial number. I'd like to get out my catalogues before I tell you anything else about it."

Nobody else argued. Longarm said he'd see them all again at seven and left for the Western Union. As he did so, Deputy Haydock tagged along to say, "You was right about Dodge City Dillon. I owe you for the bounty on Scribe Henderson as well. Who do we get to wire for money *now,* Longarm?"

Longarm laughed and said, "Another lawman named Laughing Raven, up to the Crow agency. I doubt he'll even offer to buy us a drink, by the time he's through. I'm asking him to do a sort of disgusting chore for me, unless I've guessed wrong about haunted battlefields."

Haydock looked confused as he said, "Only battlefield up that way would be Little Bighorn. You surely ain't out to find out who murdered *Custer,* are you?"

Longarm smiled grimly. "Not hardly. There's a gent called Rain-In-The-Face who's been confessing to killing Custer, personal, for years, even if other Indians do say he's full of shit. The point is that all the killing up that way took place four or five years back, like the massacre in Bad Draw. I ain't got time to go into an even older mystery about a man who walked around the horses one time. But I feel it's about time I found out whether Maxwell Windsor really walked around the horses, see?"

Haydock replied, "Not hardly. I'm sure you feel you're talking sense, but you got me confused entire."

Longarm said, "All us lawmen was *supposed* to be confused entire, by a mighty slick master-mind. And I, for one, feel it's about time we put an end to this foolishness."

Chapter 15

It was just about noon, three days later, when Long-arm strode into the lobby of the Palace Hotel in Denver, with a carpetbag full of paper and more material evidence, to find his superior, U.S. Marshal William Vail, waiting for him in a mingled state of agitation and confusion. The shorter, older, and fatter Billy Vail was usually agitated. He didn't get near enough exercise behind his desk up in the Denver federal building these days. He'd been making up for it by pacing the marble floor of the hotel lobby and, as he ran over to Longarm, he said, "You're on time today. But where in the hell have you been in all this *meantime?* You wired us Tuesday that you'd found the mortal remains of Maxwell Windsor half cremated along with his red river cart, and here it is Friday. Miss Mary Lou Windsor and her agent have to get back East for the probate hearing, now that you've proved the man dead, and here they are, still stuck upstairs."

Longarm said, "I know. Suite 603. We'd best take the hydraulic elevator up. It would be a hell of a climb. I called the meeting here, semi-informal, because I knew they was close to the Union Depot. We still got some loose ends to tie up before anyone catches a train. There ain't that much of a hurry, in any case. Maxwell Windsor died intestate. So the Surrogate back in New York City may not get around to sorting out the estate for some time."

As they rode up together in the slow but steady Otis cage Billy Vail said, "Oh, Lord, I can't wait to see the bill you run up for us with Western Union *this* time! How did you find out the man left no will afore he came West, damn it?"

Longarm replied, "By Western Union, like you just said. I had to wire the New York Bar Association to get the name and address of Windsor's lawyers. They was sort of surprised his agent hadn't mentioned them to us. Anyway, he must not have expected to get killed out West, because he never filed no will with them."

Vail thought and decided, "The daughter still gets the bulk of the estate unless it's contested by somebody closer, right?"

Longarm shrugged and said, "Don't look at me. I ain't no lawyer. There's other blood relations in the Virginia tidewater country, but old Windsor hadn't writ to them for years."

The elevator stopped. Longarm opened the gate with his free hand and they got out. Billy Vail led the way to Suite 603.

Inside, they found Cedric Smithers catching up on his own pacing while the girl sat on a settee near the window. She got up as they entered and rushed over to Longarm, sobbing, "Oh, where have you been, and is it really true about my poor father?"

Longarm sat the carpetback on a handy table against one wall and opened it as he told her, "I'm sorry to say we found his remains more than once, ma'am. The bones I found near Leaning Rocks and wired about in unseemly haste was a flimflam. I have it on the professional authority of a dentist that the skull was that of a gent no older than twenty-five. Likely an Indian, from the condition of the teeth and the shape of the skull. I'd say they found some Indian's bones whilst they was burying one Maxwell Windsor in the old Lakota campsite along the Little Bighorn."

All three of them stared at him. Smithers said, "That's ridiculous. Have you forgotten you traced the man, alive, as far south as Basin Township?"

Longarm said, "I was supposed to. Just the same, the Indian Police dug him up just a short ride from the Crow Agency and, since the body was only buried, not burned, there was enough left to recognize, even after six weeks in the ground. I fear that in hindsight I should have wondered how come an easy-going artist left portrait sketches, free, at the agency, and only left an old landscape with a landlady just as nice in Hillsboro.

"But he and his party stayed with her in Hillsboro just the same," protested Billy Vail. "You wired me they had."

Longarm took some photographic prints from the carpetbag as he said, "You mean I wired you that I'd talked to witnesses who *thought* Windsor and his party passed through Hillsboro. I really slipped up, there. I got sidetracked, talking about other matters with their pretty landlady and, well, I never *showed* her any of these pictures. I didn't have this morgue shot of the late Mason Crabtree with me, that early, anyways."

As they crowded around, Smithers snapped his fingers and said, "Crabtree, of *course!* I told you I was sure I'd met him in the art business, remember?"

Longarm said, "It might have helped if you'd remembered the name sooner. It took me, a smart Chinese, and some detective pals back East some serious thinking to figure out who he might be. But here he is, in the dead flesh. You'll note I left one the way he looked when I shot him. I had a young photo-retouch gent doctor this other print up with a spade beard. As you all can see, he don't really look like the late Maxwell Windsor when you hold their pictures side by side, but they *describe* about the same, and the resemblance is close enough to account for my suspicion I'd seen that crook's face somewhere before."

Billy Vail held the two prints side by side, nodded, and said ,"Yeah, it works. You're saying the real Maxwell Windsor was murdered just as he was starting out, and that this other gent took his place to flimflam us with a false trail leading far and wide from the real scene of the crime, right?"

Longarm nodded modestly. The girl was staring up at him in dawning horror. She said, "That's crazy, Custis! You were there when poor old James told us my father left him with those mean ranchers, south of that last town. I know for a fact that *he* was no imposter! He'd been with us for years!"

Longarm nodded. "He told me he had to be, since there was no way an uneducated man of color could get a better job. But that ain't saying he *enjoyed* being a servant. I know I sure wouldn't, and every man has his price. The so-called guide, Johnny Two-Hats, had a back-East record, too. So, in sum, a shady New York art dealer, a crooked breed who'd done time in a New York prison, and a New York servant who aspired to better things out of life, teamed up to flimflam us, as Billy says, by making it seem a famous artist had vanished miles and miles away from where they simply done him in."

Vail asked, "What was the point of them leaving the colored man in bondage like that, then?"

Longarm said, "That was an accident. How was

they to know them trash whites was almost as crooked as they? The plan was for us to find poor, faithful James waiting in vain for his kind master, one hell of a ways off from where they'd buried him. They couldn't have expected anyone to sell him into *slavery* at this late date. Had the plan gone as it was supposed to, Nate Jukes would have carried James into town after a spell, looking to get paid. James would have played dumb darky, fed everyone that story about his master on the way to Leaning Rocks with that suspicious breed, and, sooner or later, someone would have searched around there, suspicious, and found what I was supposed to find. They didn't know what a suspicious cuss I *really* am. So they figured the watch and any old bones would do it."

He glanced at Smithers. "James told me there was dozens of canvases in that red river cart. I found more than enough framing nails to buy that. But, if it's any comfort, they was naturally blank ones. Your client didn't get much painting in before they murdered him way up north."

Smithers said, "That's not important, now."

Billy Vail growled, "The hell you say. Sorry, ma'am. It's been my considerable experience that, while total lunatics may kill just to be mean, a crook with the money and brains to recruit a whole gang has to have some *profit* in mind. They *did* steal one of the poor man's paintings, right here in Denver, and if they wasn't after others, what *was* they after?"

Longarm said, "Money, of course. Maxwell Windsor wasn't just talented, he was rich. But let me chew this apple a bite at a time for you, Billy."

He took one of the arrows from Bad Draw from the bag and said, "I really got lucky with this arrow. A schoolmarm up in Basin ownship not only figured it wasn't Indian, but, once she studied it good, found the maker's lot number on the shaft. The paint had been worn or mayhaps sanded off. But she'd shot arrows back in college as a girl and, since she was sure this was the same make of arrow, she kept looking. The young gent from the photographic studio was able to bring the lettering out with some fancy chemicals. When we wired the maker, they wired back they'd surely sold said arrows, both of them, to a school-supply distributor back East. The teacher said she only had her one old yearbook from Vassar, but she suggested that the main library in a big town like Denver might have yearbooks from the fancier Eastern schools on hand. So that's where I was this morning. Guessing the right year or so wasn't hard, and narrowed it a heap. So let's see where I put the one yearbook I borrowed, and—*Grab* her, Smithers!"

But the art agent hadn't expected the gal to bolt for the window instead of the door any more than Longarm had. So she slipped by him, screaming like a banshee aboard a broom, and when she got to the window she just kept going, glass and all.

The three men ran as one to the window and looked down. She was smashed on the glass-littered pavement, six stories down. Longarm said, "I knew she was impulsive. But I figured she'd at least wait until I got to the end of my story."

Once the mangled remains had been put on ice, the Denver police as well as Marshal Vail and the bewildered Cedric Smithers wanted to know how the rest of it went. Longarm leaned his rump on a desk in the front office of the Denver morgue, lit a cheroot, and began, "You copper badges can catch up when you get your copy of the official report I fear my boss, here, expects me to spell just right in triplicate."

Billy Vail growled, "Henry, at the office, can worry about the spelling and carbon paper. You'd just accused that gal of being someone other than

Mary Lou Windsor when she took a header out the window. I'd say that more or less proved she felt guilty about *something*. But what ever happened to the *real* daughter?"

Longarm shrugged. "I wasn't able to find out, and I doubt we'll ever know. The girl went wild and ran away years ago. I suspicion Hazel Brewster and her father had her down as dead. It's easy for a wild young gal to wind up dead in such a wicked town as New York City."

Vail frowned and said, "Back up. Who the hell is Hazel Brewster?"

Longarm said, "You mean *was*, past tense. You saw her dive out the window as I was about to produce her old class yearbook. She was almost five years older than the real Mary Lou, but she acted young and innocent enough, in public, to get by. *She* was an only daughter, too, and her widowed mother died up in Boston Town the same year she graduated from college as an art major and, guess what, the captain of their archery team."

Cedric Smithers protested. "You have to be mistaken. I've known Mary Lou Windsor, my client's daughter, for years. And if you're talking about those arrows someone shot at you, she arrived in Basin Township after me, and *I* hadn't arrived when that attempt was made on your life."

Longarm said, "I'll never get finished if you boys keep butting in. All right, Smithers; you've been Windsor's agent no more than three years. Windsor's wife had died and their real daughter had run away before you ever knew *anybody*. As for who was where, when, I just showed a picture of Hazel Brewster to a ticket agent at the Union Depot and, as I hoped, he recalled selling a ticket to such a looker, lots earlier than she owned up to, when she came out of cover up yonder. She was laying for me in Bad

Draw ahead of time. She didn't arrow me, but she did silence a confederate I'd captured. Johnny Two Hats had been killed as well. It must have calmed her nerves some to notice how dumb I was when she finally chose to brazen it out and see if I'd accept her as the real thing."

He took a drag on his smoke, let it out, and said, "Trust me on such petty details so's I can wind this story up, damn it. As I was saying, Hazel Brewster come down to New York to be part of the artistic world. She met up with old Maxwell Windsor, likely as a model, and one thing led to another until she was living with him as his mistress. Windsor was a good old boy, but a mite reclusive. He didn't have close friends he might have had trouble fibbing to. He didn't want to marry a play-pretty young enough to be his daughter. I can't say I blame him. But people will talk, even in the artistic world. So they decided to pass her off as his long-lost Mary Lou. One pretty little thing looks much like any other, when nobody's seen either for three or four years. Living together that way, they naturally wound up in a few family photographs, along with faithful James, who had to be let in on it but saw no reason to give the show away in front of company. She couldn't have known, until she got here, that an earlier portrait of the *real* Mary Lou was hanging on the wall of a Denver art gallery. Or that, worse yet, the very lawman answering her pathetic plea to find her dear old dad had *been* to said art gallery, asking specifically to see said picture. She had no way of knowing I just wanted to see some of the missing painter's work and accepted a blurry picture of a much younger gal as close enough."

Vail said, "That could account for the attempts made to stop you from ever meeting the fake Mary Lou. And I can see how such a sneaky gal would have a motive for wanting a sugar daddy who wouldn't marry her probated as her real father. But it was still dumb of her to go out that window, Longarm. For the house of cards you've built so far is mighty circumstantial."

Smithers said, "He's right. Proving she was his mistress instead of his daughter doesn't prove she was in on it with the people who actually murdered poor Maxwell. He was missing, after all, and even a kept woman has the right to report her keeper overdue for supper."

Longarm reached in a pocket and drew out the singed watch as he muttered, "I was hoping I could hold out on this particular evidence. It still runs, on twenty-one jewels, and I was told I could get a new case for it, reasonable."

He handed it to Vail, who opened the case to examine it. Then he said, "The same smart jeweler up in Basin was able to help me trace that fancy watch to its point of sale at a fancy shop on the New York Ladies Mile. Their engraver was able to recall the date an unusually beautiful young gal had asked him to engrave such an unusual inscription. I'll allow even a naughty gal has the perfect right to bestow a fine watch on any man she may choose to. But she bought that watch and had it engraved so sentimental a few days *after* she reported her poor father lost, strayed, or stolen."

Billy Vail whistled softly. "That would have been a problem to explain in court, even if she could *prove* you'd compromised yourself as the arresting officer. Is that why she quit trying to kill you, but the way?"

Longarm smiled sheepishly. "I'd like to think she got sort of fond of me, near the end. But she was likely using me the way she used other men. She made some deal with Crabtree to fund as well as run the operation until she could split the estate with him. Being a crook to begin with, Crabtree had no problem with the heavy work. The gal and old James was just out to flimflam us. Save for that one impulsive time she tried to play wild Indian in Bad Draw."

Smithers said, "Hold it. I can't say who might or might not have tried to get you with a bow and arrow. But have you lost count of the time she shouted that warning on the railroad platform, when Crabtree and that hired gun had the drop on the two of us?"

Longarm shook his head. "I keep saying she was sort of impulsive. Greedy, too. And even if she didn't see a chance to grab the whole pie, then and there, Crabtree was about to mess up. She yelled, 'No, don't!' To *him*, not *us*, and, just the same, wound up in business for herself."

He flicked ash on the bare floor and explained, "She had no choice but to meet me in person and brazen it out after she missed me with that arrow. When she saw I thought she looked as much like a Mary Lou as a canvas smeared-up, years earlier, with a putty knife, she saw I was as good or better to her alive than dead. Once I'd bought her story and even rescued James for her, she valued my hide even more.

"How much of your hide did she get at?" asked Vail dryly.

Longarm said, "Don't try to butter me up with flattery, boss. I *said* I'd put all this down on paper, later. What she valued me *most* for, by then, was that I'd been fed the story that would lead me to the discovery of her poor old daddy's mortal remains, and likely testify for her when the estate was probated. But she had no way to tell Crabtree of her change in plans. He still had plans to kill me before I got wise. In a way, I reckon he was smarter about me. He didn't know old James was using my room at the hotel. They murdered him by accident. That left all her confederates but Crabtree and Dodge City Dillon out of the picture. When we was kind enough to deal *them* out of the game as well, she must have felt mighty pleased with herself. For, had I wrapped things up the way I was *supposed* to for her, she'd have wound up with *everything,* free and clear."

Vail said, "I assumed she felt sort of upset when she dove six stories. I'm proud of you for having such a suspicious nature, Longarm. Let's go back up to the federal building now, and get all this down on paper."

Longarm protested, "Hell, boss, it's a Friday afternoon, and it wouldn't kill you to let me knock off a mite early, would it?"

Vail said, "Our office stays open until after five and it ain't three yet, you rascal. How do you know that widow woman up on Sherman Avenue would be available this early in the day, anyway?"

Longarm said, "I wired ahead, and I been stuck up in a cowtown three whole nights, Billy."

Vail laughed despite himself. "Not alone, if I know you. Was that schoolmarm you mentioned as so helpful good-looking?"

Longarm looked hurt. "You sure have a dirty mind, Billy Vail. Poor old Molly Compten is thirty if she's a day, and she has her reputation as an upright pillar of the Basin community to consider."

So Vail said he'd only been funning. Longarm told him he was forgiven and that they would say no more about the expensive timepiece in his pocket if he could just be on his way now.

His boss laughed, and told him to get out of his sight before he changed his mind, and naturally Longarm never even mentioned that prim little schoolmarm up in Basin Township to the Junoesque widow woman waiting for him up on Sherman Avenue.

It would have been against his code, even if sweet Molly Compten hadn't made him swear he'd never tell a living soul where he'd spent his last three nights in Wyoming.

Watch for

LONGARM AND THE BLOOD HARVEST

**one hundred and eighth novel in the bold
LONGARM series from Jove**

coming in December!